FALLING FOR THE KNIGHT

ENCHANTED FALLS BOOK TWO

CECELIA MECCA

ALTIORA
PRESS

S axford Castle, Northumbria, 1394
"Your decision, my lord?"

The thief held Tristan's gaze. This man's death, or even his excommunication from Saxford, would cause hardship for his wife and child.

"Lord?"

Tristan turned his attention from the thief to Gerard, the look he offered his steward ensuring there would be no further interruptions. He understood the man's desire to see these men out of their hall—it had been a long day—but he would not be rushed.

"You understand," he said to the cowering accused, "that the merchant's loss was substantial? Your life could be forfeit to pay for it."

Tristan watched the man's eyes as he blinked and finally looked at the merchant whose cloth he'd stolen. He had heard the thief's plea for mercy—he had a new son—as well as the merchant's demand for retribution. Looking at both of them now, he finally came to a decision.

"Aye, my lord. I understand."

"Consider yourself grateful, then, to work for the merchant any time he passes through Saxford. Whatever he needs, for a period of five years, you will offer him. And if you are caught relieving anyone of their hard-earned goods again, your son will be without a father."

Tristan waited for the judgment to penetrate and was neither surprised nor affected by the merchant's confusion and the thief's cries of thanks. He motioned for Gerard to usher the accused and accuser from the great hall and sat back in the wooden chair that had become mighty uncomfortable.

Tristan tilted his head back and closed his eyes. He waited for the inevitable, knowing it would come any moment. Three, two, one . . .

"A punishment of service?"

"Gerard, I'm tired—"

"'Tis unheard of. The cost of the cloth—"

"Which was returned."

"I should not question your judgment—"

"Then don't." Tristan was hungry, tired, and in need of a woman. He'd returned from the border that morning to learn the manorial court would be held that day. A timely return for the thief, who may have lost his hands or his life had Gerard been his judge.

By the time Tristan opened his eyes, a stream of men-at-arms and servants had already replaced the petitioners who'd sought his judgment. They'd been waiting for the court to end so dinner could be served. He stood from his chair, which would be moved behind the head table for the meal as the trestle tables were moved from their positions along the walls and arranged in the center of the room. Gerard followed him out of the hall and away from the preparations.

They were about to enter the covered passageway that led to the south tower when Gerard stopped and looked back.

"I'd know the outcome of your trip, but Lorelle—"

"I tire of your fawning, as well as hearing her name. Bed the woman and be done with it."

His trusted advisor and longtime friend was not amused.

"She is not the kind of woman—"

Tristan's head began to ache. He rubbed his temple. "She's unmarried."

"Aye, you know she is."

"And willing."

"We've not discussed—"

"Of course you have not. Lorelle," Tristan said, "is neither married nor titled. So—"

"But she is the kind of woman—" Gerard interrupted.

His head was getting worse. "Do not say it."

Gerard did. "That a man could marry. I've been considering—"

Tristan did not mean for his laugh to be quite so derisive. "You have gone daft, old man."

In truth, Gerard was only one year his elder. And at three and thirty, the steward was not exactly close to the grave. But if he thought to bind himself to a woman, one woman, for the rest of his life, then his friend and advisor must truly be losing his memory.

Gerard ignored him. "I promised to assist her—"

"There you are."

Tristan turned to the newcomer—Walter, Saxford's marshal—whose quick breaths indicated he had been running. He'd never seen his marshal in such a state of agitation.

"What's wrong?" Tristan asked. He only realized he'd unsheathed his sword when both men looked down at it. From Walter's expression, Tristan guessed it would not be needed, so he returned the broadsword to its sheath. Their enemy had not come for them yet.

"There's a woman," Walter said in a rush of words, "along the shore."

Tristan and Gerard exchanged a glance.

"A woman?"

"Aye, my lord. Lying along the shore. We do not know if she is dead or alive—"

Tristan didn't like Walter's expression. Why did the man look so worried? A lone woman lying along the shore should not pose a threat. "How could you not know if she's alive? How did she come to be there?"

Walter shook his head. "I know not, my lord. But none of the men will approach her."

"What is wrong with them? With you?"

The man took a deep breath. "She is . . ."

His marshal's evasiveness was not improving the pain in his head. "What in the name of—"

"Her attire." Walter shrugged. "'Tis odd. And the men are afraid she may be some sort of witch."

He was finished with this nonsense. Before Walter finished speaking, Tristan turned and made haste toward the shore. A witch. Though he did not personally believe such nonsense, some of the men were quite superstitious. He could hear footsteps behind him, but did not slow his pace toward his horse, which was already readied for him. A woman with odd attire? Had the marshal been hit in the head? What attire could possibly have frightened the men so?

Reminded of the pain in his own head, Tristan prayed he could be finished with this matter quickly. He had more important things to worry about, like the end of the truce and, more pressingly, his rumbling stomach.

HANNAH BREATHED in the salty air and concentrated on the sound of distant seagulls with relief.

She was home.

Back in Mayport Bay, no longer in Scotland somehow, but home—

Except . . . she wasn't.

When she opened her eyes and finally focused, it took only the briefest of moments for her to realize this was not Maine and she was most certainly not at her family home. She sat up, her joints as stiff as if she were ninety-eight rather than twenty-eight.

What the hell?

The castle looming above her was what had given it away. The only castle she knew of in New England was the one in New Hampshire where she'd attended a wedding once. What was it called? Did it really matter? She'd somehow ended up on a beach, alone, instead of—

Caroline? Allison? Where were her sisters?

Heart racing, Hannah tried to stand, but a wave of dizziness forced her back onto her sandy seat. It came back all at once. The waterfall. Their jump. She'd been pulled under, and while she'd expected to float up toward the surface at any moment, it hadn't happened. There'd been a brief moment of panic before . . . nothing. There was nothing after that but darkness, and now this beach.

How had she come to be here? And where were her sisters?

Too weak to stand, Hannah put her head in her hands, trying to piece it together. They'd left the inn late for their hike to Leannan Falls, the driver profusely apologetic for having been caught in traffic. She had been uncharacteristically quiet, staring out at the rolling hillside and thinking about the end of their trip, and had only piped up when Caroline first broached the subject of cliff jumping.

Allie, her more practical, saner middle sister, had immediately objected. There was no way either of them would jump off a cliff. Hannah was afraid of heights, and she'd only agreed to hike the falls, not to jump from them. And yet somehow, less than two hours later, she had joined hands with the only two family members she had left in the world and jumped.

Where in God's name were they?

"Hold!"

She spun around, her eyes widening.

"Stay there," a man yelled from his horse. The vehemence in his voice startled her. It was as if she'd done something wrong. He had three companions, all on horseback too, all lined up behind her as if they'd been there awhile.

Hannah made another attempt to stand, and the man in charge, or at least she assumed he was in charge, rode toward her.

"Hold!" he yelled again, dismounting.

She blinked in confusion. All four men were dressed up in medieval garb. The one in the lead was older, probably over fifty, but his companions all looked younger.

The most likely explanation was that they were reenactors, employees from the massive castle perched along the edge of the nearby cliff. After nearly two weeks in Scotland, she'd seen more castles than she had during a lifetime in the States.

The States.

She was already beginning to think like a European. The thought might have amused her if not for the men gathered in front of her. They looked absolutely appalled.

Hannah's hands began to tremble as she struggled to make sense of it all. As her head cleared, panic began to set in.

"Where am I?" she asked.

"Do not move," he repeated.

She'd heard some thick accents in the past few weeks, but his was positively dripping. Hannah could barely understand his English.

"My lord will speak to you—"

"My lord?" she interrupted. "You mean the owner?"

Dumb Hannah. The owner was also likely a lord. Was this one of those castles that people still lived in when it wasn't being traipsed on by tourists like her? But why would the owner want to speak to her? Was he pissed that she was trespassing?

Hannah didn't get scared very often. She was the strong one, a role that was more important now than ever. But there were exceptions, of course, like when she was in a tall building looking down. Or, God forbid, on a Ferris wheel or something of the sort.

Jumping off a waterfall and waking on an unfamiliar shore certainly qualified for that list. Hannah's hands couldn't stop shaking and her heartbeat pounded in her ears.

"Who are you?" the man demanded.

He looked like an older version of that tour guide from Inverglen. Bearded and shaggy, what you'd imagine a Highlander to look like. Though, to be fair, most of the Highlanders they'd met didn't look much different from most men. Well, other than the ones who wore kilts . . .

Focus, Hannah. Something is not right here.

"Who are you?" she demanded back.

Her question seemed to startle them as much as her appearance obviously had. It was a simple question really. And why were they looking at her as if she were wearing a clown suit? Hannah followed their stares to her shorts and hoodie. You'd think she wouldn't need it, this being July and all, but one thing she'd learned quickly about Scotland was that summer didn't always mean warm. Especially now that she was completely drenched.

Hannah took off the only relic she had of her alma mater, with the exception of her college loans, which would never let her forget that she'd chosen a Yale degree, and began to wring out the gray sweatshirt. Until she caught their expressions.

"OK, what is going on?" she demanded. Hannah was beginning to feel a bit more like herself despite the fact that she was still completely lost with no recollection of anything after jumping into the falls. "You've been less than helpful. I have no idea how—"

The men turned at the sound of a few approaching riders. Literally, riders on horseback, dressed similarly to the others. They sped toward them like bats out of hell. The one in the center was huge. As the others stopped, he just kept riding. Closer and closer . . .

Was this maniac going to stop?

He finally did, jumping from the biggest horse Hannah had ever seen in her life. He stalked toward her as if he meant to kill her. When he got close enough that Hannah could see his features, she swallowed.

Holy hell. If this guy was a reenactor, then she was joining their troupe tomorrow.

2

*T*ristan had never seen anything quite like the woman who stood in front of him. He moved toward her for a closer look. He understood now why his men acted as if they'd seen a selkie. But while she was wet from top to bottom and clearly disoriented, she was nevertheless very human.

His eyes lingered on her shapely, nearly bare legs, clothed only in a pair of short, form-fitting braies, before he forced his gaze upward. Her dark hair clung to her shoulders, framing a perfectly shaped face. Full lips made for kissing. Eyes a clear, crisp blue so startling against her olive skin that he could imagine staring into them for hours and never becoming bored. His eyes dipped to the strange garment bunched in her hands.

"What are you?"

It was the most ridiculous question he could have asked. Surely she was a woman. And yet, she was also something more . . .

"Excuse me?"

"Where are you from? Your accent—"

Blinking and taking a deep breath, she asked again, "Where am I?"

"Are you injured?"

"I . . . I don't know."

Had she hit her head? The only time Tristan could remember anyone acting this disoriented was after a head injury. They could be dangerous, fatal even. He lowered his hand to her head without preamble and, as gently as he could, began to feel around for a bump or wound that would explain her condition.

"What are you doing?"

He ignored her and continued checking her scalp. Nothing.

"Why are you all dressed like that?" she asked. "Do they have that Society for Creative—"

"Who are you?" he demanded in a tone that should have provoked an answer.

Instead, she raised her chin. "OK, so you're owner of this place? I guess you're in the middle of some kind of . . . reenactment. I didn't mean to interrupt you. But will you please tell me where we are? I need to find my sisters. I need to get back, our flight—"

"I can't understand your words." She spoke so fast and many of her words were completely unfamiliar. Tristan switched to French and repeated his question.

"I don't speak French," she said.

Tristan didn't know if he should lock her in his dungeon . . . or his bedchamber. A fascinating woman to be sure. But until she was a bit more forthcoming about how she'd breached their defenses, he had no choice but to detain her.

He reached for her wrist, deciding on the spot he'd have to question her himself as the men seemed to be—

"Get your hands off me!"

Tristan had expected resistance. Not to be kicked in the leg. He'd never met a woman so bold.

"God's bones," he muttered, "be still—"

"Get. Your hands. Off me."

Though she was clearly terrified, his captive spewed venom with her words and her eyes. Anger had darkened them from their usual ice blue.

Tristan reached down and patted her sides, attempting to ignore the curves beneath his hands. No weapons.

"What kind of person treats a tourist this way? Do you honestly believe—"

"Tourist?"

He repeated the word as he mounted, indicating the others should go ahead of him. "I will take her," he said, pulling the woman up in front of him before she could object. With a loud "Umph," she landed nearly in his lap.

They rode toward the castle, the gentle slope dotted with tall grass and rocks. This well-worn path was the only one that led to the shoreline, and with Castle Saxford the only building for nearly a half-day's ride, Tristan still could not understand how she'd come to be here. Or where she'd come from. He'd never before believed in witchcraft but . . .

"Where are you taking me?" she demanded, attempting to push away from him. Did she not realize a fall from here would break her neck? Tristan shifted, attempting to put more distance between them. Inadvertently, he inhaled deeply, and her scent was intriguing enough that he leaned closer to smell her hair again.

"Did you just smell my hair?"

"How did you get down there?" he asked.

Without warning, she reached down into the pocket of her odd braies, something he'd never seen a woman wear before today, and pulled out a black rectangle. She looked at it and used a most unladylike epithet.

"Dead. Of course," she muttered.

When he halted, his men did the same.

"Go," he said. "I will be along."

Though they looked reluctant to follow his orders, the others rode ahead. He watched them ride around the east tower and toward the gatehouse. Reaching down, he snatched the item from her hands before she could protest.

"Hey, what are you—"

"What . . . is this? And why did you say that it had died as if it were an animal?"

It was hard to the touch, shiny on one side and smooth on the other, and completely unlike anything Tristan had ever seen.

"I really need to get this in a bowl of rice."

He had no idea how to respond to that.

"What . . . are you serious? You're telling me you don't have cell phones here? It doesn't seem that remote. Edinburgh—"

"Edinburgh," he repeated, pronouncing it the correct way. She was certainly a foreigner, but from where?

"Whatever. We aren't that far away, and—"

"We are more than two days' ride from Edinburgh," he said, still looking at the black box. It was smooth and shiny, like the side of a black rock. But with indentations on its edges.

"Two days' ride? You mean drive? How is that possible? It took less than an hour to get to Leannan Falls, and we must be near there, right?"

She'd turned to look at him, her eyes wide again. He looked down to where her shirt clung to her very prominent breasts. What matter of costume was it that she should reveal so much?

"Ahem."

He looked up.

"OK, what the hell is going on? Did you kidnap me from Leannan or something? If so, you are the worst kidnapper in the world. And what's with the outfit?" Her voice increased in pitch as she spoke.

"Kidnapping? Do you take me for a reiver?"

"A . . . what?"

Tristan's headache was returning with a vengeance. Had he not been so tired and hungry and out of sorts, he might have had a bit more patience.

Handing the odd object back to her, he said, "You will stay at Saxford until I can determine how you were able to breach our defenses. And you will explain your odd attire and—"

"'Odd attire'?" She gasped. "You show up looking like some guy from Medieval Times and call *my* 'attire' odd? I don't know what the hell is going on, but I'm sick to death of it. The last thing I remember is jumping into that waterfall. I need to find my sisters, especially Caroline so I can wring her pretty little neck for making us do something so stupid. But I most certainly can't stay here." She nodded to the castle. "I have a flight to catch tomorrow. So"—her eyes narrowed —"will you please tell me where I am and who you are so I can get back to the inn immediately?"

Remarkable. He hadn't understood everything, but there was no mistaking her tone, somewhere between derision and fear. Though he knew plenty of men who'd have tossed her back onto that beach by now, Tristan was not the sort to shy away from a challenge. And she was most certainly going to be just that.

He spurred their mount forward and responded, though surely she must know more than she pretended to. Unless she really had hit her head and did not realize it.

"You are at Saxford Castle—"

She shook her head. "No, that's not possible. I saw that on the map. That's in England."

"Northumbria."

"I thought it was Northumberland? And we can't be in England."

They'd reached the gatehouse. Tristan looked up to the guards, who immediately opened the portcullis. His companion stopped talking as they passed through the thick stone walls. Once they reached the courtyard, they were greeted by his new squire, who had clearly been waiting for him.

"Durwin," he said, dismounting and reaching up to help —"What name are you called?"

She wasn't looking at him. In fact, she wasn't looking at anyone. Whereas she'd been arguing with him the moment before, her eyes were now closed. And if he hadn't been there to catch her, his guest would have fallen and broken her neck. She slid right into his arms, limp and motionless.

"Is she dead, my lord?" Durwin's eyes widened, with good cause.

He leaned down and felt her breath on his cheek.

"Nay, Durwin, she is not."

"What is she wearing?"

He knew not. Nor did he know where she came from, or what strange manner of an object she carried in her hand. But Tristan was determined to find out.

FOR THE SECOND time that day, Hannah struggled to remember where she was. It felt as if she were being—

"Where are you taking me?"

The brute from the beach was carrying her over his

shoulder, her head facing his chest, as if she were a bag of flour. She was still in this strange place, with this strange—if handsome—man. The memory of the courtyard they'd just ridden through slammed into her. It had looked like something out of the Middle Ages. Boys playing with wooden swords, horses being led into a stable, people dressed like servants scurrying around. For a moment she'd actually thought she'd left the twenty-first century.

Ridiculous.

"Please put me down."

They were climbing up a stone stairwell lit by torches in brackets. It finally occurred to Hannah that she was in serious trouble. She was in a bizarre place in a foreign country, far from the waterfall, if he told the truth, with no recollection of how she'd come to be here. Her lack of memory implied she'd been roofied, but if this man had abducted her, why had she woken up alone on the beach?

"Stop!" she screamed, her hands shaking as she struggled to get away from him. His face and body were almost too perfect, but that didn't mean he wasn't an axe murderer. She punched him in the chest, though it was like punching the stone wall that surrounded them. Surprisingly, he *did* put her down, and she promptly scrambled up and away from him. Sitting on the stone stair, she tried to catch her breath. Hannah had never had a panic attack before—not even her parents' deaths had induced what her best friend described as 'a night terror in the middle of the day.' But she knew the signs well and was pretty sure it was happening to her now.

"You need to lie down."

"I need to know where I am and what is going on," she managed to say.

Hannah could not catch her breath.

"You really don't know where you are?"

Why did he seem so surprised by that? And why did he

talk so strangely? He thought she had an accent, but he sounded like a cross between a British actor and her Latin professor in college when he was trying to impress the class.

"Please. Please tell me what is happening. Why is everyone dressed like that?" She indicated his medieval garb. "Who are you?"

Her kidnapper looked awfully sympathetic for someone who had orchestrated such an elaborate scheme.

"I am lord of Saxford Castle—"

"Right. And why is everyone dressed up?"

His eyebrows drew together as he continued to stare at her. "Let me take you abovestairs—"

She was dreaming! This did feel very real, but there was no other explanation. Maybe she'd hit her head in the jump from the falls, and this was all a long fever dream, like with Dorothy in *The Wizard of Oz*.

"I'm dreaming," she said, finally able to draw a deep breath.

"What do your parents call you?"

"My parents?" They didn't call her anything. Not since last year anyway. What an odd way to ask her name. "My name is Hannah," she said, pinching her arm. Ouch! So that trick apparently didn't work.

"Hannah?"

She looked at him again. Of course! Where was she likely to meet a tall man with the physique of a Highland hero if not in a dream?

"Hannah Sutton." She might as well play along. "From Maine. My sisters and I went to Scotland to honor our mom and dad's wishes. You know, take the trip they were never able to take. Except Caroline decided a simple hike wasn't enough for our last day. She convinced us jumping into the falls would be the perfect way to start a new chapter in our lives. God, if only she hadn't read *Alice in Wonderland* too many times as a kid. New chapter, my ass."

He was looking at her as if she had a screw loose. Perhaps she did. Hannah was sitting in a circular stairwell, after all, talking to a man who was likely a figment of her own imagination. But what other explanation was there? When he'd first ridden into the courtyard, she'd thought they were in a different century.

Which was, of course, ridiculous.

"I need to leave," she said, less and less convinced this truly was a dream. The smell of roasted meat drifting down the stairs seemed very, very real, and the stone beneath her was convincingly cold. Which meant she was back to square one.

He didn't respond. Instead, his eyes narrowed. "Hannah Sutton." He said her name as if it were a curse. "You are not leaving until I know how you came to be here."

She stood, exasperated. "I told you, I have no idea how I came to be here," she said, mimicking his formal speech.

"What is this?" He pointed to the cell phone she'd taken out of her pocket before remembering it was dead. "And where is this Maine you speak of?"

Oh God, she really had no time for this. Light from the closest torch caught her eye, and it occurred to her that this whole place was a major fire hazard.

"Is that safe? Oh, never mind," she said when she saw his puzzled expression. "Maine. The United States. In the Northeast, near Canada."

He stared at her blankly.

"You don't know what a cell phone is. You've never heard of Maine—"

"United States?"

OK, so this guy was definitely some kind of nut. Too bad. He really was quite good-looking. Fearsome, but hot.

"Listen, I don't know what game you're trying to play—"

"My lord?" The boy who'd greeted them earlier, before Hannah fainted like an eighteenth-century heroine, peered his head around the curved stretch of steps beneath them. "Is she well?"

"Quite," the lord said dryly.

"Dinner is served. Walter and Gerard are inquiring after you. Shall I tell them—"

"I will join them momentarily."

"Very good, my lord."

When he scampered back down the stairs, Hannah stared after him.

"Is there some kind of festival here or something?" She had to give it to them. Their devotion to the illusion was admirable and their costumes were superb. In fact, she had planned plenty of themed events, but never one quite this authentic. The attention to detail was amazing. Whoever designed the costumes and décor should be commended. The very first event she ever planned after starting the business was medieval-themed, but compared to this, her own seemed more like a kids' birthday party.

"Festival?"

"Like the one at Alnwick Castle. Is that why everyone is dressed up?"

The man looked at her as if she were speaking a foreign language. "What cause did you have to be at Alnwick Castle?"

Hannah laughed then. In fact, once she started, she couldn't seem to stop. The events of the day were suddenly just too much.

Except the look on his face was so serious. This guy who looked and acted like he was from the Middle Ages wasn't just messing with her. He'd never heard of the United States. Or cell phones. But wouldn't that mean . . .

Of course, that wasn't possible. Hannah turned and ran

before he could stop her. She followed the smell, up and up, until she came to a landing. She ran down a corridor, hardly noticing her surroundings, until she reached an archway.

Hannah took one look inside the hall in front of her and froze.

TRISTAN NEARLY RAN INTO HER.

And for the first time since this strange encounter had begun, he was genuinely worried. The look on her face was one he'd never forget. Preparations for the meal were nearly complete, and though he spied nothing unusual, she certainly seemed agitated by the scene. He couldn't explain why he felt the need to protect her, but he did.

Grabbing her arm none too gently, he led her back to the stairwell and then up to the next floor. That she did not protest told Tristan what he already knew. He'd seen that look on the battlefield plenty of times, though it usually came just after a man caught his first glimpse of a few hundred mounted, armed knights sitting across the open field.

He'd planned to bring her to the constable's tower, but instead he guided her to a wall-walk outside the keep that led to the great chamber. The others knew she was here and would be looking for him. But he needed answers first.

He opened the door to the chamber where he'd laid his head these past ten years. Tristan moved to a trunk, pulled out a woolen cloak, and handed it to her. She really should remove those wet clothes, but he didn't think she'd be amenable to the suggestion. He led Hannah to a wooden chair, its plush red velvet cushion one of the remnants of the former lord, an Englishman whose extravagance had known no bounds.

Grabbing a pitcher from a table next to it, he poured goblets of wine for them both.

"Drink."

Surprisingly, she listened.

"Did you remember something?"

She shook her head but didn't answer.

"Do you know why you're here? Did Sutherland send you?" It didn't seem likely his enemy would use this woman to kill him, and when she looked at him with the same vacant stare with which she'd regarded the hall, Tristan had his answer.

Already finished with the wine, she placed her goblet on the table next to her.

"What year is it?" she asked.

So she had injured her head after all. He suspected from the look on her face that she'd not listen to him, or answer his questions, until she had answers of her own. So he stopped trying for the moment. "The year of our Lord thirteen hundred and ninety-four."

"And I am in England?"

"Saxford Castle, Northumbria, just south of the border."

Hannah took a deep breath, let it out and frowned, the creases at the corners of her mouth not marring her beauty in the least. All the ferocity and fight in her appeared to have bled away. The change in her, frankly, worried him.

Ignoring the knock at the door, he said, "Tell me. Everything."

She opened her mouth but didn't speak. The look she gave Tristan told him she didn't trust him. Nor should she. But she had no other choice.

"Let me help you. I would not presume to hurt an innocent woman, no matter her manner of dress. Or speech."

"You would help me?" The vixen who'd kicked him with such conviction on the stairs sounded almost plaintive. It didn't fail to move him, and he found himself saying, "Aye, I would."

"Dry clothing." She looked down at the fur-lined cloak. "I could use some dry clothing please."

This he could not manage on his own. But he knew who could. "Done."

"And I need to get back to Leannan Falls as soon as possible."

With war on the horizon, his men would be particularly suspicious of her—her motives, her strange clothes and words—and Tristan knew too little about her to allay their fears. But either she was the least-trained spy he'd ever met, or she was in need of his assistance. Though he had many questions for her, he had no doubt she was genuinely panicked and confused. No one could feign the kind of response she'd had in front of the hall.

"You said it is near Edinburgh?" He'd not heard of the place himself, but as long as it was not on Sutherland's property, bringing her there should not be a problem.

She nodded.

"Will you eat first?"

Again, she nodded.

Tristan stood. "I will be back," he said, turning.

"Wait!"

She'd made to come after him but stopped abruptly when he looked back at her.

"No one else can see me like this," she said, opening the cloak.

"Where is this 'Maine' where they wear no clothing?" If she didn't close the cloak, Tristan would do it for her. He really did need to find her something she could use to cover herself.

"Italy."

He was so distracted, Tristan forgot his question.

"Maine is a small village in Venetia."

"Italia?"

Tristan had never been there himself, but he'd met enough Venetians to know this was most certainly not how they dressed.

Why does she lie?

"I will find clothing," he said finally, "if you promise to tell me the truth."

He nearly laughed at her confused expression. She was not a very good liar.

"You may pretend not to understand, but if you care to return to your falls, then you must think of a better lie than that. Or the truth will do. Either way, I will have answers."

Before she could open the cloak again, Tristan left to seek Durwin, only to find his trusted squire awaiting him outside the door.

"Who is she, my lord?" Durwin said in a hushed voice. "The men say they found her on the shore, lying there—"

"Listen to me, and listen well," Tristan said. "You will tell no one of the woman's arrival. Do you hear me?"

"Aye, my lord."

"And find Joan. Tell her to come immediately."

"The laundress, my lord?"

Rather than answer, Tristan gave Durwin a moment to think about how few females served at Saxford and how many of those were named Joan.

"Aye, my lord." Durwin bowed and hurried off to do his bidding.

Such a good lad. Tristan was about to go back inside, but his hand froze above the iron handle of the door. The ten-year truce was coming to an end in less than a month. Tristan had a battle to prepare for, and there would be a visit from his ally Lord Kenton any day now. He had no time to play nursemaid to a woman who'd washed up on the shore and could hardly keep her wits about her. Tomorrow, he would send her north with an escort and be done with it. In the meantime, he would keep watch on her himself, just in case he was wrong and she had been sent here as a spy after all.

Either way, he'd be rid of her soon. A shame, for his mysterious woman really was quite comely. He did not know how much time had passed that he'd been thinking of the beautiful stranger when Joan came upon him suddenly.

"My lord, you sent for me?" The laundress rounded the corner much more quickly than he'd expected her.

"There is a woman inside my chamber." He ignored Joan's frown. "Not that kind of woman." But as soon as he said it, he thought of Hannah's long, bare legs and imagined them wrapped around his waist.

"My lord."

Joan had served at Saxford longer than Tristan had been lord here, and she'd been one of the first of the previous lord's servants to accept him. For that he owed her his gratitude, but not an apology for his wayward thoughts. So he continued instead, "Find something suitable for her to wear. Assist her in preparing for the meal."

In the meantime, he needed to find the rest of the men who knew Hannah was here so he could ensure they kept that knowledge to themselves.

"Lord . . ."

He'd already turned and left Joan to her duties. "I must go—"

"But, my lord, what manner of woman is she?"

He stopped. *I know not* would not be an acceptable answer, though it had the benefit of being true.

"A lady," he said finally, not believing his own words. No lady would ever expose herself as Hannah had done, and yet she had not seemed ashamed by her lack of clothing. No common woman spoke to a lord as she had either. Without anything more to offer, he turned to leave.

He could feel Joan's gaze on him still, but Tristan could not explain what he did not understand.

But he did intend to get answers as soon as Hannah joined him at the meal.

3

*H*annah stared at her folded hands. This could not be happening.

"My lady?"

She looked up at Joan, unsure of what the older woman was asking. Hadn't she done everything that had been asked of her? Indeed, she'd allowed herself to be trussed up like a Thanksgiving turkey without so much as a word, which was not like her at all. If her sisters could only see this gown, its long sleeves that nearly touched the ground and soft, deep-green velvet that felt as luxurious as anything she owned . . . But what could she possibly say to the woman? That the outfit looked like a costume and she suspected she may have traveled back in time some six hundred years?

No, that was a risk she didn't want to take. The guide on one of the castle tours she and her sisters had taken had insisted women weren't burned at the stake for being witches in medieval Scotland. Even if it was true and witch hysteria hadn't begun until the sixteenth century, she wasn't taking any chances.

"Shall I escort my lady to the hall?"

Joan reminded her of the housekeeper her parents had hired just before they died. Hannah had only met her once on a weekend visit, but her kind face and ever-present smile had made her immediately likable.

"I suppose," she said, trying hard not to be ungracious. Though her stomach roiled and her hands could not stop trembling, Hannah stood and followed Joan from the bedroom. Or whatever this monstrosity of a room was called. The only time she'd ever seen a bedroom this big and ornate was on a tour of the mansions in Newport, Rhode Island. It was easily the same size as her apartment and half the size of the house where she'd been raised.

She followed Joan back outside onto the wall-walk, and as they passed the courtyard, Hannah stared down at it with wide eyes.

How could she truly have believed Tristan and his men were playacting? Her mind must have known before she did. Preservation?

There was no way all of this could have been recreated. Just as before, men were sparring down below. Other people bustled back and forth, dressed in everything from armor to what amounted to glorified flour sacks, their garments stained and worn from real use. A wagon filled with hay . . . chickens and pigs mingling with their owners.

She was going to faint again.

Hannah stopped and held onto the stone wall lest she topple over the side.

"My lady, are you well?"

"No," she managed. "No, I am not."

Oh God, please do not pass out again. The scene below blurred and Hannah called upon the yoga classes she'd taken in an attempt to steady her breathing. Another panic attack? Please, no.

Is this even possible?

Time travel was the stuff of science-fiction novels, not real life, and it certainly shouldn't be happening to her.

Well, then how do you explain—

"Hannah?"

When she looked up, Tristan stood next to her. Where had he come from?

Looking at the sword strapped to his shoulder, it suddenly struck her that he was an actual, honest-to-God knight. A lord of some sort. And she'd been so rude . . . She was lucky he hadn't ordered her execution or something. As an event planner to the rich and famous, she was accustomed to dealing with powerful men. And yet, she had not acted as she would if she knew he was a lord. The even-keeled Hannah who would have been much more deferential gave way, nearly the moment they met, to the feistiest one reserved for friends and family.

"I'm fine," she said. A blatant lie. "I am just slightly afraid of heights."

That much was true.

"Indeed," he said, watching her. The wave of nausea left, and her breathing had returned to normal. He'd changed, and his hair was damp. It looked darker now, less blond than brown. And short. The other men had much longer hair, and nearly all of them were bearded. *His* beard had been shaved to heavy stubble. His lips were full for a man, and really, she should not be staring at his lips. She'd traveled through time for God's sake!

Her lie about Venice hadn't convinced him, of course it hadn't, but it was the first thing that had popped into her mind. She clearly was not English, and she didn't speak French. At least she'd been to Italy before, twice. But she hadn't thought the plan through.

She didn't speak Italian any more than she did French.

"Hannah, you need to talk to me. I can't help you otherwise."

"I'm sorry if I'm not inclined to accept help from a man who detained me against my will."

"I worried you might have been a spy for Sutherland."

Now it was her turn to be confused. He'd mentioned that name before, and it had meant as little to her then as it did now.

"A Scotsman," he clarified. "Our enemy."

"Our?"

"He is an enemy to my overlord, and therefore, one to Saxford as well."

"I see. And you no longer think I am also your enemy?"

This time, his gaze was slow and deliberate as it raked up and down her body, leaving a tingling sensation in its path. Right now, it didn't matter that he was a knight or a lord or her captor. He was just a man—and she wanted him to kiss her.

Hannah! Seriously?

But those lips . . .

"Nay, I do not," he finally said. "Though I would like to know what you saw in the hall that scared you. And why you lied about being from Venetia."

Shit.

"Sei straordinariamente bella."

Yeah, this wasn't going to work. Sometimes she really did wonder how she'd managed to squeak her way into Yale as a graduate student.

Wait . . . bella. She knew what *that* meant.

"Let me help you," he pressed.

Part of her wanted to tell him the truth, yet she knew she could not. She wouldn't have believed it herself had there been any other possible explanation. He'd either be afraid of her and think her a witch or decide she was mad.

I just need to get him to take me to the waterfall.

If Caroline and Allie had been transported too, they'd find a way to meet her there. And there had to be a way for them to get back home. If the falls had sent them here, they could send them back too. Some way.

"I . . . I can't tell you."

He crossed his arms. Even with a shirt and some padded coat-looking thing with a crest on it, Hannah could tell he was heavily muscled.

"Look, I really can't. I just need to get back to Leannan Falls. I was with my sisters when . . . when I must have hit my head or something. Maybe someone took me and dumped me on that beach. I don't know. But I have to find Caroline and Allie."

He knew she wasn't being completely straightforward with him. If only she'd realized earlier what was happening, maybe she could have come up with a more plausible story. One time Hannah had stepped on a glass Christmas ornament, her mother's favorite, and sliced her foot. She'd taken off all of her clothes before anyone could find her. Literally. Every single stitch. To this day she didn't know why—her mother said she must have been in shock. But her sisters still teased her about her literal inability to think on her feet.

"I will send you there with an escort." If Leannan Falls was anywhere near Sutherland's land, he'd be signing his own death warrant if he brought her himself.

"Then what does it matter—"

"It matters because . . ." When he took a step toward her, Hannah did not move away.

"Maybe I can help."

"And why would you want to help me?"

He shrugged. "Because you need it."

He seemed so genuine. She was still concerned about the whole witch thing, but something told her he deserved her honesty. Surely this was another really, really bad decision, but she was going to do it.

"I am from Maine, like I said originally. In the United States. You don't know of it yet. Apparently some Vikings may be there, but it won't be until the late fifteenth century—actually, more like the sixteenth century—before the English are involved—"

"Hannah, what in the bloody name of Saint Thomas—"

She took a deep breath, liking this idea less and less. Unfortunately, she'd never been much of a poker player. She had no choice but to see it through.

"The twenty-first century. I am from the twenty-first century."

The look on his face was exactly what she would have expected, so Hannah talked fast.

"My sisters and I came to Scotland on the one-year anniversary of my parents' death. They died in a car accident —you wouldn't know what that is, but . . . never mind. We were supposed to go home tomorrow and wanted one last sightseeing excursion. We'd heard Leannan Falls had some kind of 'healing properties.' Of course, I didn't believe that, but Caroline, that's my youngest sister, can be pretty persuasive. And not only did we go to the falls, but she convinced us to jump in. Like a Three Musketeers thing, one for all . . . you don't know that either. Anyway—"

"Hannah—"

She was losing him. "Please listen to me," she begged. He did want to believe her, she could tell that much. He looked like a client who didn't have the money to spend on his event but really, really wanted to hire her anyway. "We jumped. I was terrified, but we did it. And then I woke up on your beach."

She let that sink in.

"I thought at first you were role-playing for some event,

or maybe showing off the castle by donning your best medieval garb."

Oh God, he didn't even know what *medieval* meant.

"When I saw the courtyard . . . I could hardly believe it. I never pass out. Never. But maybe it was my mind's way of preserving me, kind of like if you go through a trauma or something and then can't remember it afterward. I don't know. Anyway, the more time I spent here, the more it struck me that the level of detail was just . . . unbelievable. And the torches. And the way you all spoke as if—" she laughed, "—as if you were from a whole different time."

The concerned furrow in his brow had grown deeper with every word. He thought she was certifiable.

"And you hadn't heard of things like the U.S., or a cell phone, and something just clicked. It sounds nutso, I get it. And part of me still wonders if I'm dreaming. But I pinched myself, more than once actually, and—"

"Another time?"

"The future, to be precise."

She took a deep breath and waited.

Please, please believe me.

SHE NEEDED A PHYSICIAN. Or perhaps a healer. For all Tristan knew, only the priest could help her. A shame. So beautiful and yet . . .

He'd become impatient waiting for her, so he'd decided to check on her and Joan—only to find her on the wall-walk. It had taken him a moment to recognize the beauty in the green gown. Where had Joan managed to find one that fit so well? Where had Joan managed to find a gown that fit so well on such short notice? Though its long, wide sleeves were no longer in style, the color suited her. He'd have preferred her hair down, but Joan had pulled it back with one single braid encircling her head. She had the face of an angel, the sharp eyes of an intellect, and the enthusiasm of a young girl, though he thought she was probably not much younger than him.

And she was also quite mad.

"I think perhaps—"

"You don't believe me. I can tell." She reached into the small pouch hanging from her belt and pulled out the strange black box he'd examined earlier. "This"—she waved it at him —"is a cell phone. Take it."

He would do no such thing.

"Look," she said, shoving it into his face. "You can make phone calls on it. That is . . . speak to people in other locations. But it's dead. From the water."

Tristan really needed to get that healer.

She put it back and took out another item. Before he could stop her, Hannah took his hand, opened it, and dropped something into his palm.

It was a thin, flat rectangle made of some strange slippery material with raised markings on it. He turned it and attempted to read the markings.

"A credit card. See, my name is there. And that's plastic. I'm surprised it stayed in my pocket. You won't see that for a few hundred years. You can use it to buy things in my time. It's like money. Coins."

He turned the card over in his hand for a long moment before giving it back. Tristan leaned against the parapet. Dusk was just beginning to set, and the meal he'd looked forward to was likely well under way. He wasn't sure what to think. But the idea that she'd fallen into a waterfall and traveled back through time . . . He'd heard of such fanciful tales but had no use for such things as magic and faeries. Only the real world interested Tristan.

"The Black Plague," she blurted.

Her intent expression told him that, if nothing else, she really did believe what she was saying.

"All of the people that died."

"The pestilence?"

"I guess," she said. "We know it as the Black Plague. It was a pandemic spread by rats on ships."

"Rats," he repeated.

"Your war with France—"

"Is over."

She shook her head. "No, it's not. They call it the Hundred Years' War in my time. It will begin again, and France will win."

"You cannot know such a thing. How is it possible—"

"Because I am from the future." She shook her head. "It sounds as crazy coming out of my mouth as it must sound to you. But I'm not nuts, and I'm telling you the truth."

"Hannah, do you understand this is not possible?"

She was frustrated, though no more so than he. For some reason he wanted to believe her, but this strange fancy of hers could not possibly be true.

"Tristan, or lord whatever, *please*. Take me to the waterfall yourself. Maybe there will be some way for me to prove this to you. And my sisters—"

"Did they travel through time too?"

"You don't believe me."

"I do," he lied.

"No, you don't."

"Come with me to the hall. Eat. We will talk more later. I can send for the—"

"No!" She swallowed. "Sorry, I meant to say, please do not tell anyone else what I've told you."

"As you wish. I will not send for the priest, but my men

33

found you. They saw your . . ." Her clothing. It was unlike anything he'd ever seen. "I need to tell them something."

"Yes, they saw my shorts. They're called shorts. And a T-shirt. And my Yale hoodie. That's where I went to graduate school. That is . . . university."

Tristan nodded. She was right—telling the others was not advisable. Though they were unlikely to believe her, they might decide she was some sort of danger. "We will need to think of another story." He thought for a moment and then landed upon the perfect solution. "The Swan."

She would not like it, but it would work.

"We will say you are from The Swan. That you took a dram and found your way to the beach instead of the gatehouse. Throughout the years, many women have come here looking for me. Some, unfortunately, come looking for coin." He smiled. "And some come for other reasons."

It was damned inconvenient, being reminded of his previous life.

"It will explain your poor manners," he added. The furrow in her brow indicated she was not well pleased by that. "A lady would not speak as you do." His explanation only seemed to make her angrier, so he hurried to finish. "But it will do for the night. And we will talk about your escort later."

"What," she asked, clearly agitated, "is The Swan?"

Pleased with the plan and his quick thinking, Tristan smiled. "A stewhouse. Or more precisely, my mother's stewhouse, when she was alive."

She clearly had no idea what that meant. Tristan tried again.

"A bordello."

Hannah's eyes narrowed. "A brothel? You want me to pose as a whore?"

Tristan had already turned to walk away.

a bsolutely not.

She had a mind to stay where she was, but the promise of food compelled Hannah forward. Following Tristan into what appeared to be the largest of three towers connected by the walkways, she entered through a door that her host had to duck to use. Once inside, she realized they had simply taken a different route to the great hall. Unlike the ones she'd seen on her tours of Scottish castles, this one was three floors above the ground.

And this one was in active use.

Most of the other great halls she'd seen had been empty, full of crumbling rock, and in Alnwick Castle, the one place the Sutton sisters had visited in England, there'd been several empty tables. All of the people changed the atmosphere entirely.

Conversation died away as she followed Tristan into the cavernous space. The food smelled even more inviting than it had earlier, when the meat was roasting, but that was the only familiarity here. Men and the occasional woman crowded about the tables, eating with their hands. No, that was not precisely true. Some used knives, though the blades looked big enough to gut a deer. No butter knives here.

Hannah had always imagined the Middle Ages to be dark and drab. But nothing could be further from the truth. Color burst from every crevice. From the lively costumes—no, outfits . . . these were no actors—to the wall hangings, bracketed torches and candles made the hall as bright as a sunroom in June.

When Tristan halted in front of her, she nearly ran into him. He leaned down to whisper, "You cannot sit with me. Not as a—"

"I am not a prostitute," she whispered back, keenly aware of the attention focused on them. "Nor will I pretend to be one. So think of another story, or let me do it. But I absolutely refuse—"

"Come," he said, walking away again. The man had a tendency to give orders, and it was beginning to grate on her. She'd never allowed herself to be treated as lesser in the twenty-first century, and she wasn't about to start now. That wasn't how you got ahead in business or in life.

She followed him to the raised dais at the back of the hall. A long table and four large wooden chairs sat on it, the carvings on the chairs meticulous enough to make a woodworker weep.

He pulled a chair out for her, the gesture not one she'd expect from a man like him. Hannah sat and looked down at the crowd. She lifted her chin, refusing to feel self-conscious. She might be out of her element—hell, a few hundred years out of her element—but her business had required her to become a chameleon. If after being raised in a small town in rural Maine she could rub elbows with some of the wealthiest members of the Boston elite, she could certainly be accepted here.

"Ignore them," Tristan said from the chair beside her.

"It's not them," she whispered, though she was grateful some of the people in the hall had already returned to their meals.

"Something is amiss."

She looked up at him. Even seated, Tristan was a good deal taller than she.

"What if I can't get back?" she whispered.

He looked as if he was about to say something in response, but a man approached the dais. "Lord Saxford, my apologies."

Hannah recognized him as one of the two men who had been with Tristan at the beach. What the heck was in the water here? Although this man was a few years older than Tristan, he was also not displeasing to the eye. If you liked beards.

"I'm told you were looking for me?" the man continued.

"Gerard, you've met Lady Hannah. My lady, Gerard is the steward here."

Steward? How does one address a steward?

"Good evening, sir," she said, deciding to err on the side of politeness.

"Lady Hannah." He nodded the way a CEO would nod to one of their employees. He clearly wanted to ask about her but didn't. Interesting. Was that because of Tristan's position? Or were the manners of this time not so different than her own?

"We will speak later," Tristan said. "I do need to talk to Walter. Is he dining in the hall this eve?"

Gerard had started shaking his head before Tristan finished speaking. "Nay, my lord. He has already retired. His stomach . . ." The man seemed reluctant to finish.

"Very well."

Gerard bowed and left, giving way to a young man of no more than fourteen or fifteen. The boy placed what appeared to be a flat piece of bread in front of them and filled it with some kind of meat. Another boy followed him up onto the dais and filled both of their cups. So much for the idea of the serving wench.

Tristan looked at the food in front of them and then at her. Was he waiting for something?

"My lady."

"My lord." Hannah nearly laughed at how funny the words sounded coming from her lips. But the fear that she might never see Maine, or more importantly, her sisters again, kept her from doing so.

He gave her a quizzical look and nodded down to the meal.

At a loss, she finally asked, "Am I supposed to do something?"

Tristan sat back and crossed his arms. "You truly do not know?"

Hannah had never been known for her patience, especially on an empty stomach.

"Maybe you didn't hear me earlier, but—"

"I heard you." He uncrossed his arms and leaned forward. "It is customary for a lady to eat first when she shares a trencher with a man."

"Trencher?" She looked down as soon as he said it. He could only mean the 'plate.'

"Why?"

"Hannah, please eat."

She did not have to be prompted twice. Mimicking her dinner companions, she ate a piece with her fingers. The meat was so heavily spiced she nearly choked on it. But she forced it down, not wanting to insult him.

He followed her lead, and after a few bites, Hannah became a bit more accustomed to the spice. Until she remembered the reason they'd spiced the meat so heavily in the Middle Ages . . .

She was going to be ill.

"You don't like it? Saxford's cook—"

"No," she said, much too quickly. "It's delicious."

No refrigerators.

She couldn't do it.

Thankfully, the servant had returned with another tray. This time, he placed it on the table between her and Tristan. Cheese. That should be safe. And figs. Hannah picked up one of each.

"Refrigerators," she whispered. The closest table to them was not very far away, and the last thing she needed was to be overheard talking about refrigerators in the fourteenth century. "In my time, we have . . . boxes, of sorts." She was not prepared to explain electricity. Instead, she said, "And they keep things cold. Like meat."

She'd give it to him. Though Tristan clearly did not believe her, he did not recoil from her words. He looked at her as if she were a curious specimen. That is, until she licked her finger clean and he began looking at her in a completely different way . . .

This language, it would seem, was the same across the centuries. She could have been sitting in a bar in Boston, except none of her boyfriends had looked remotely like Tristan—and they'd possessed none of his staggering confidence either. She'd dated an attorney once who worked for one of the largest firms on the East Coast. But even he had not exuded the sheer power and control of a man who was literally lord of his own castle.

"How does the son of a . . ."

Crap, how to say it delicately?

"Bawd?" he offered.

Tristan lifted a silver goblet toward his lips and she rushed to do the same.

"Pardon?"

"My mother was a bawd. She owned the most prominent stewhouse in South Derbridge, just outside of Berwick."

"Right." The wine was honestly not bad. She was more of a beer drinker and typically disliked red wine, but this one was really good.

"You're wondering how the son of a bawd becomes a knight?"

"Well, yes. Or a lord. I thought there were strict rules about that. Defined classes. And primogeniture and all that."

"At times, I find myself wondering if you truly are from a different time," he said. "I speak three languages and have never heard of many of the words you use."

"Three languages? I've always admired that about Europeans. Most Americans only speak English."

"Americans?"

"My country. In any case—" she took another sip, "—it's unusual, right?"

"Nay, it is not common for someone like me to be sitting here." He indicated the dais on which they sat. "But neither was my mother common. Most houses such as The Swan are owned by either married couples or the church."

Hannah nearly choked on a fig. "The church?"

He appeared amused by her surprise. "Aye. It is a profitable business, and one which keeps the vices of men contained."

The church. Her Roman Catholic mother would have been appalled to learn such a thing, if it were indeed true.

"The year she died, she had enough coin to donate a new altar to the church."

"She donated an altar?"

"My mother was a religious woman. Never missed mass,

although it took years for the church officials to permit her entry."

She had so many questions.

"By the time I was ten and two, she'd saved enough coin to persuade the local armorer to accept me as his apprentice. Four years later, our work was noticed by the Earl of Kenton."

For the first time since they'd met, Tristan didn't look so hard, as if he were about to cut someone down at any moment. He'd clearly loved and admired his mother. The notion that this man, from a time when women had no rights to speak of, valued strong women made him more appealing.

"In exchange for our exclusive services, the earl agreed to train me."

"What kind of services?"

"Helmets," he said, taking a bite of meat.

She did the same, waiting for the rest of his tale.

"The armorer who trained me specialized in helmets."

"And you were that good?"

This time, there was no mistaking his slow, sensual grin. It would appear the double entendre was alive and well in the Middle Ages. "I am."

She might be stuck in another century, but she could flirt with this hot medieval knight, couldn't she? Why the hell not? Hannah could flirt with the best of them.

"Am? So you are still an armorer then?"

He held her gaze. "Nay."

"Then you are good at other things, I assume."

"Very many things." His voice was low and seductive. She swallowed and looked away, wondering if this was a game she could not win. Getting pregnant by a man from another century was not a part of her plan for the future.

"As I said . . . ," he continued.

She dared to make eye contact.

"I was raised in a bordello."

Visions of his perfect body naked on a bed surrounded by women, teaching him how to . . . dear Lord. But then the reality of his statement hit her. If he were raised in a brothel . . . were there diseases in this time too? Likely.

She looked away again. This was why she could never be a politician. No matter how hard she tried to lie or equivocate, her face always told the truth.

"Hannah?"

She took a sip of wine, pretending to be composed, before slowly turning back to him.

"Yes, Tristan?"

"Do men and women make love in your United States?"

Had he seriously just said that?

Well, she would see his bold statement and raise it with one of her own.

"Sex," she said, letting the word drip from her lips. "We call it 'having sex,' and yes, they do have sex. Though it's not considered polite to discuss it so openly. For strangers, at least."

"Hmm."

What the hell kind of response was that?

They both returned to their meals, Hannah watching in fascination as servants moved efficiently through the tables. There must be nearly fifty people in the hall, maybe more. It was like a small restaurant.

"Sex."

The word so startled her that it took her a moment to realize Tristan had spoken.

"I like that word," he said.

And Hannah smiled, knowing she had him.

"I do too."

HE SHOULD HAVE ALLOWED someone else to escort her. Had he done so, he wouldn't currently be struggling with two insistent thoughts as he led her to her chamber.

First, he wished he were bringing her to *his* chamber, but the rule he'd set for himself years ago precluded it. Having seen so many of The Swan's women forced into uncomfortable situations, he'd vowed to never be the one to initiate 'sex.' It had rarely been a problem for him, but tonight . . . tonight he would have likely broken his own rule if given the chance.

Second, though he still did not believe Hannah was from the future, Tristan could tell she truly believed she hailed from this United States, and from another time, an impossibility for a woman who otherwise appeared quite healthy.

His beautiful visitor was quite a mystery.

He came to a stop outside her door, but neither of them moved. Damn, he wanted to kiss her. Instead, he cleared his throat and said, "Your chamber awaits, my lady."

"Thank you for allowing me to forget everything," she said. "Even for a few moments."

When she blinked up at him, Tristan's cock demanded his attention. Taking a deep breath, he attempted to ignore his body's response. Another reason the idea he was now contemplating would not do. No matter how much he longed to spend more time with Hannah, he could not be the one to take her to the falls.

And yet . . .

"It was my pleasure," he said, surprising himself with the sincerity of his own words. Despite, or perhaps because of, her strange mannerisms and speech, he had enjoyed their conversation.

Still, he did not move. And when Hannah finally turned toward the door, he surprised himself again. "Nay . . ."

Her hand paused on the iron handle, and the urge to pull

her away from the door, to draw out their evening together, almost made him break his own vow.

The smile she gave him would have tempted a priest.

"Your time," she said, her voice like the thick velvet she wore. "Is very different than I imagined it would be."

When his foot took a tiny step forward, Tristan caught himself and moved it back.

Come to me, Hannah. Reach toward me, and I am yours.

"Is it better or worse than you imagined it would be?"

Better. Say better.

"Neither," she said instead. "It is simply different." She lifted her chin. "*You* are different."

She took her lush bottom lip in her teeth, the gesture shooting straight to his cock. She was going to kiss him. He willed it with his entire being, told her with his eyes how good their lips would feel pressed together.

"I am a simple lord. No more."

This time, her smile was the same as it had been when they'd bandied words at dinner. Tristan braced himself for whatever she was about to say.

"You are anything but simple, *my lord.*"

And with that, she turned and pushed the heavy door. When he took a step toward her to help swing it open, her sweet scent filled his nostrils. Then, just before she closed the door behind her, Tristan caught her glance. The unmistakable look in her eyes would haunt him for the remainder of the evening. It was the same expression he likely wore himself.

Regret.

She did not want to leave him yet, and neither did he want her to go.

Tristan had his reasons for not acting on the powerful desire that consumed every bit of him, and it would seem Hannah had reasons of her own.

5

*T*ristan rubbed his temples, the pain in his head from earlier returning. He sat in the room over the gate, his customary meeting place with his marshal. John, his new sergeant, was also present for the meeting. The man had come to Saxford after his old lord was killed in battle, and they were grateful for it. His horsemanship skills were celebrated on both sides of the border.

"I need to get back—"

"To your visitor?" Walter asked. He sounded genuinely concerned, and Tristan couldn't decide if he was grateful or annoyed.

He'd hated lying to his most trusted advisors, but there had been no choice. Hannah's version of the truth was not acceptable, and she'd rejected his story about The Swan. So he'd spun a story that clung to the truth without being true. Traveling alone was more acceptable for widows than unmarried ladies, so he'd claimed she was a widow. Her wits were addled, likely from a fall, and she remembered only that she'd been traveling with her sisters and had become separated from them at Leannan Falls.

"Aye," he said. "To arrange her escort. Have either of you heard of the falls?"

The men exchanged glances.

"Nay," Walter said.

"I have," John said, "but you won't be pleased to learn where it is."

"Tell me." Though he already suspected what the answer would be.

Walter and John exchanged glances.

"It's located on the very edge of Sutherland's property, just north of its southernmost border."

Damn. That would not do.

"We can't take her there," Walter said. "Any provocation now—"

"Provocation?" His patience with the Scottish border lord had come to an end months ago. When Kenton granted him this property, the one closest to his most bitter enemy, he had promised to protect it. Even if that meant being more patient than was comfortable. "He has threatened to attack us the moment the treaty ends. If anyone is provoking—"

"Are you prepared for battle now? I despise Sutherland more than any man alive, as do you, but if he were to attack now—"

"We will be ready."

They would need to be. Rumor had it the wardens did not intend to intervene, which meant there would be another bloody border war that would see men dead on both sides— all for a feud none of them had started. But he'd sworn to protect the people of Saxford, promised as much to his over-lord and the man who pulled him from a stewhouse to a new life, and so he would.

"My lord," Walter pressed, "if a contingent of men is caught anywhere near—"

"I will ensure it does not happen."

"Also," John said, his gruff voice filling the room, "there are strange rumors about those falls."

He stood, wanting to get back to Hannah.

"I care little for rumors."

With his hand on the iron door handle, Tristan was about to leave when John's words stopped him.

"Aye, but the men must be careful." The warning was rather vague and obvious, but something about John's tone gave him pause.

He turned. "Aye, of Sutherland—"

"Nay, of the falls."

Every hair on his arms stood on end.

"My sister says a faerie lives in the pool beneath the falls."

"A faerie?" He laughed, chiding himself for having given the rumor even a moment's consideration. Tristan did open the door then, bidding farewell to his men.

Faeries existed only in children's tales, and were even less believable than time travel. Even so, Walter and John were right. After nearly ten years of peace, he couldn't be the one to break the treaty with Sutherland. It would expire on its own the following month, and when it did, a battle would be coming.

And he was prepared for it.

HANNAH PACED IN THE BEDCHAMBER, as she now knew it was called, that she'd slept in the night before after Tristan had left her hot and bothered. Her tossing and turning most of the night had little to do with her predicament and everything to do with the man she nearly lost herself to on the doorstep of this chamber.

She'd awoken this morning to the comforting thought that it had all been a dream—only to open her eyes and find herself here, dressed in the potato sack of a nightgown Joan had given her. A fresh wave of panic had washed over her, and nothing short of seeing those falls would help. To think she'd been worried about catching her flight. Ha! She was pretty sure airlines would not exist for hundreds of years.

With nothing to do but wait, Hannah studied the bed she'd slept on. She supposed the oversized frame would be called a four-poster bed back home, though Hannah had no idea if those words would be used here. The mattress was stuffed with feathers, or so she imagined based on how it felt. Surprisingly, the blankets, or coverlets as Joan called them, were as soft as the bamboo ones she'd recently purchased for her room in Boston. The stone walls were covered with colorful tapestries, expensive-looking ones, though she was no tapestry expert.

Joan had appeared not long afterward with a tray of food and a change of clothes. The 'lord' apparently thought it best she eat here, alone, rather than disturb his hall with her presence. She honestly didn't care. Frankly, being surrounded by men who looked as if they'd jumped off the pages of a medieval encyclopedia unnerved her. Here, at least, she could pretend she had not somehow traveled back through time in that waterfall.

Healing properties indeed.

A knock landed on the door, which was opened before she could respond. Her breath caught in her throat at the sight of his big body filling the entire entranceway. Tristan was dressed much as he'd been the day before, in thick woolen hose and a cream linen shirt layered beneath an armless jacket-type thing.

Hannah shivered.

"I see Joan has found you another gown?"

This one was much simpler in style than the blue one she'd worn to dinner. Joan had insisted on a slip . . . no, she'd called it a chemise, but Hannah hadn't really seen the purpose. This gown, though cut quite low in the front, covered every other inch of her. But she'd relented, not wanting to raise any questions.

"She has," Hannah said, spreading the material out around her feet. How did women get anything done in these? "Whose gown is this?"

Rather than answer, Tristan came inside.

"It doesn't matter."

She knew from Joan that Tristan had never been married. Saxford had lacked a mistress for the ten years he had been lord here. Hannah had been about to ask about the previous lord when another servant had come looking for Joan. Apparently, she was the laundress here too.

Hannah hated laundry and couldn't imagine doing it without a washer and dryer, especially given how much fabric was used in each gown.

Which got her to thinking about the other things that had not been invented yet. How was she supposed to live without computers? The internet? Instagram? She forced herself to stop that particular train of thought. She was going to find her sisters and get home. Somehow. Staying here was not an option.

And yet, the first question she found herself asking was, "What do you call a girlfriend in your time?"

"Girlfriend?" Tristan took another step inside and closed the door behind him.

Her body didn't care about the fact that she was six hundred years and a few thousand miles from her home. With every step he took toward her, Hannah struggled to slow her rapid heartbeat. "Girlfriend. Boyfriend. Someone that you date. Actually, you don't date, come to think of it, do you? People just get married, right?"

"I don't know this word, date."

Finally, he halted his advance. He definitely did not smell like she'd have expected. While she distinctly remembered one of the guides talking about medieval people's lack of hygiene, he smelled quite nice, like pine. A scent she never imagined would smell quite so . . . sexy. What else had they gotten wrong?

"When a man and woman . . ." Hannah had never been shy. But man, this guy flustered her. "Get to know each other. Before they marry. Or maybe they don't."

"Have . . . sex?" he said with a smile. "Is that what you mean?"

"Never mind," she said, trying to dismiss the whole topic. What had she been thinking? If she was lucky, she'd find some way to get back home. Then they'd never see each other again. "When am I leaving? Did you find someone to bring me to the falls?"

"Answer me, Hannah."

Her name had never, ever sounded so . . . sensual.

"No, that's not what I meant." Not exactly. "More importantly—"

"I will answer your question when you answer mine."

"Are you this high-handed with everyone," she snapped, knowing the answer. He was a lord, and Tristan very much acted like one.

His brow furrowed in confusion. Ugh, it was like they spoke two different languages. He clearly had no idea what she meant.

"I appreciate your help, Tristan, I really do, but—"

"Tell me what you meant by 'girlfriend,' and I will take you to the falls myself."

No. Absolutely no way. Travel with him? Hannah could barely look at him without swooning, especially after their banter last night. Besides, she'd never been the type to go for thickheaded men with six-pack abs.

"One of your men will do just fine."

His response was to make himself right at home, on her bed, no less. The temptation to sit beside him—to sit *on* him —was hard to resist.

"Nay. My sergeant has heard of Leannan Falls, and it happens to be located in an area that could prove dangerous."

Hannah tried to think back, but she really knew little of English history—and even less about this region, except . . .

She paled. Holy shit. William Wallace, Robert Bruce. Hadn't the Scottish Wars of Independence broken out along the border? When had that gone down?

"What is it?"

"Nothing," she lied. There was no point in bringing it up given how little she actually knew. "What kind of danger?"

Tristan frowned. "The kind that could get you killed. The falls are located on the property of a man who would take great pleasure in using our trespassing to incite a war between us."

That definitely sounded bad. "Why?"

She tried to move but remembered the monstrosity on her body. And to think this was the simpler of the dresses she'd worn. Hannah would be changing into her shorts the moment they left Saxford.

"I'll tell you after you explain 'girlfriend' to me."

The man was insufferable.

"Fine." Hannah tried to think back to earlier times, to bridge the divide a bit. "At one time, men and women entered into a courtship. Do you at least know what that means?"

He shook his head.

"A period when they would get to know each other before getting married."

"A betrothal."

"Kind of. But not that committed. They could still

decide not to get married. Courtship is considered kind of old-fashioned though. Now . . . well, not now, but in the twenty-first century, people just date." How to describe dating? "They get to know each other, go out, like to dinner or to a bar . . . that is, a pub. Seriously, you don't know 'pub?'" What could it possibly be called in his time? "A tavern?"

Hannah laughed at Tristan's dubious expression. So men and women did not date in taverns. "If you are dating some-one, getting to know them, but not dating anyone else, you are boyfriend and girlfriend. Exclusive. To each other."

"Married?"

"God, no!" She thought of some of the boyfriends she'd had in the past. One particular stuffed shirt was so full of himself that he actually chastised a maitre d' who addressed him as mister rather than doctor. That had been their last date. Thank goodness those arrangements had been easily broken. "Nothing that permanent."

"So boyfriends and girlfriends go to a tavern together . . . and do what?"

Hannah shrugged. "I assume the same thing you do now. Talk, eat, drink." She left it at that. "No such concept in your time, I guess?"

Tristan tilted his head. "No."

"So what do a man and woman call each other before they are married?"

"Betrothed."

"Before that."

"Strangers. Or maybe friends if the families know each other."

"Geez."

"Unless you are a whore."

Had he seriously just said that? "Pardon me?"

"There are women who have relations with men before

marriage, but they are either widowed or common. Unless they're getting paid, and then they are—"

"I know, you don't have to say it again." Hannah hated that word. "Those women are called prostitutes in my time."

He was looking at her strangely again, his head cocked to one side.

"What do you mean by common?" Widow, she understood.

"A woman who is neither a lady nor a . . . prostitute."

"Right. Because ladies don't have sex before they're married. No contraception and heirs and all."

"Is it not so in your time?"

He still didn't believe her, but at least he was playing along. So would she.

"We don't have an aristocracy," she said. "No lords and ladies or anything like that. So no, it's not like that. I mean, there are classes, but . . ."

"And what is contraception?"

Oh boy. Better just to get it out there. "Ways to prevent a woman from becoming pregnant?"

"You mean—"

"Having a babe."

He paused, presumably to think about that one for a second. "There are ways," he shrugged. "Though they cannot always be trusted."

And though neither said another word, an understanding passed between them. One that did not need to be spoken of aloud. One that would prevent her from ever knowing Tristan that way.

How had they gotten so off-topic? "Your turn to answer my question."

"I will tell you tonight." Tristan stood.

"Tonight?"

He looked her up and down, and she hated that her body

immediately responded. He was arrogant and borderline cocky. Definitely presumptuous. And yet . . .

"It's getting late."

"Late? It can't be a minute past seven o'clock . . . in the morning."

Yes, another blank stare.

"If we're going to get to Leannan Falls by tomorrow, we will need to leave soon. I've no desire to—"

"Tomorrow?"

And then it hit her. "Tristan, how will we get there?" She still wasn't sure how she felt about traveling with him, but she supposed it was preferable to a stranger. And he obviously cared little about her opinion on the matter.

"Horseback," he said as if she were daft.

"That's what I was afraid of."

6

*T*his was not how he'd planned to "take care of it." If he were found anywhere near Sutherland's property, it would give the old man the excuse he'd been looking for.

Which was why he'd decided to take her alone. If someone who did not know Tristan spotted them, they could perhaps pass themselves off as a married couple. Still, Walter and John had not needed to tell him it was a bad idea, though they had, and more than once.

"How long will it take us to get there?"

Tristan tried to ignore the feeling of Hannah's arms around his waist, concentrating instead on keeping her mounted. The revelation that she'd never ridden a horse before had nearly convinced him to believe her fantastical tale. It was obvious from the way she rode that she was being truthful. At least he'd chosen a smaller, lighter horse for the trip, one with a special ability for navigating through the mountains.

"We'll camp just over the border tonight. According to

John, Leannan Falls is at the intersection of the River Tweed and Whiteadder, so we should arrive tomorrow."

"Why did you decide to take me?"

"Does everyone in your time talk so much?"

"So you believe me now?"

Of course he did not believe her.

So how do you explain her clothing? Her speech?

When they'd left earlier this morning, Tristan had found himself studying her as she walked through the castle. She looked at it as if, well, as if it was all new to her. She reached out to touch everything, eyes as wide as a babe.

"No."

Tristan slowed when the path split into two. He knew the terrain well, and while he did not think reivers would be a problem, he wasn't inclined to take chances. They'd meet less travelers if they stayed away from Saxford Village. When he turned his mount, the top of Saxford Castle came into view behind them. He marveled that it was truly his, just as he'd done nearly every day for the last ten years.

He turned, wanting to gauge Hannah's reaction.

"It's very pretty," she said softly.

He was inclined to agree. Whatever century she was from, Hannah's wide eyes and perfectly smooth cheeks gave her a look of innocence that her expression never quite matched. A mystery, one he'd likely not solve. If she found what she was looking for tomorrow, he would never see her again.

"Thank you," he added, spurring the horse forward into a stretch of marshland.

"Yesterday you said this trip could be dangerous . . ." Hannah trailed off, her words tinged with fear. He wished he could say he'd exaggerated the matter, but he had not.

"I suppose I should finish my story. Ten years ago I was nothing more than an armorer's apprentice—"

"A position your mother had secured."

"Aye. I told you of the Earl of Kenton. He took notice of my work and eventually became our sole patron. One day, he came to our shop himself and found me attempting, poorly no doubt, to wield the small sword my master had given me."

"How old were you?"

"Ten and six by then. Most squires are already trained for battle by that age." And he'd never so much as felt the clang of an opponent's sword. "He offered to train me, and of course I accepted."

He remembered the first time he'd entered the training yard . . . the other squires and knights had not attempted to hide their scorn. He tried to remember those first days with gratitude, but those sneers had marred his memory.

When they hit a bump, she tightened her arms around him, her breasts pressing up against his back. Perhaps he should have worn armor despite the fact that he hoped not to need it.

"I see."

"Kenton and his wife were never able to have children," he said, as if that explained it. Of course, it did not. Plenty of boys had squired for the earl over the years, but Kenton had seen something special in him. "His castle was where I met Gerard, my steward. He was also fostered by Kenton." The third son of a minor baron, fostering by Lord Kenton, he'd held no title other than "sir" and no prospects other than the ones he took for himself. They'd gotten along from the first.

"So how did you come to be lord of Saxford. Or how do you say it?"

She didn't understand titles?

"Tristan, will it be this bumpy the whole time?"

Every time Hannah said his name he wanted to feel her words against his mouth. Though he couldn't see them now, he could imagine her lips gliding over his own. Their dinner conversation, and his sleepless night afterward, did little to distract from such musings.

"Aye, it will." He took a deep breath and concentrated on his story instead of the sensation of Hannah's curvy body pressed up against him.

"How did I come to be Lord Saxford? You might not believe the tale."

"Is it more unbelievable than my own?"

Tristan chuckled. "Indeed, it is not."

He slowed through a slog of mud, the marshland soon giving way up to the steepest incline they would face on this journey. If Hannah considered the ride bumpy on flat land, she would not be happy about the mountainous terrain ahead.

He gripped the reins, glad to be alone on the road, and thought back to that fateful day.

"Kenton's family and Clan Sutherland have been enemies for longer than both groups have existed. In fact, none remember the reason for the feud, only that each generation of Kentons and Sutherlands continued to raid and plunder one another with such vigor that even their allies began to abandon them. Along a bloody border, their enmity stood out as the most vicious, until the wardens eventually appealed to the kings on both sides to see an end to it."

"Wardens?"

"Leaders, on both sides of the border, to enforce March law."

Hannah was never quiet, so he assumed she did not know what that meant.

"If indeed you traveled through time, you chose a dangerous location. The border between England and Scotland has not seen true peace in my lifetime despite the laws that were created to make it so. Reivers continue to wreak havoc on the weak, nobles and clergy use black mal to line their coffers, and only men like Kenton can secure safety for their people."

"You mean blackmail? And what do you mean, men like Kenton?"

"The strongest men, the ones who can garrison themselves behind defenses—"

"Like Saxford."

"Aye."

"So what happened when the wardens appealed to their kings?"

Tristan resisted turning around. He could already see her face in his mind, sharp and expectant. He smiled. "They agreed on a most unusual way to reconcile the unrest. Twenty men from each side battled to the death. The winner claimed victory and set their terms."

"That's barbaric!"

"But it worked. Kenton slew every one of Sutherland's men."

He may have shocked her, but at least Hannah was distracted enough not to realize they were climbing to a peak that was high enough to afford them a view of the North Sea.

"So what does this have to do with you and—"

"I was one of the men who fought for Kenton."

Hannah gasped.

"I'd gone to witness the event, though of course I could not fight. Kenton's best knights had been chosen for that honor. But when one of those men ran off—he jumped in the river, if the rumors can be believed—Kenton was left one man short."

"The best knights indeed."

He agreed but remained silent.

"And so you fought that day instead."

"In front of King Richard, who insisted on attending. It was, after all, his idea—"

"He sounds awful."

The treasonous statement flowed from her as if . . . well, as if she did not understand it was treason. "When the battle was over, the king treated me as if I'd helped win a great battle even though I'd only killed two men. My first two, in fact . . ."

Tristan could still remember the sounds, so different than the clanging of swords in the training yards. These strikes were so much more insistent, loud and angry. Blood had spattered everywhere. He'd since become accustomed to the sight, but back then—

"And that's how you came to be Lord Saxford?"

"After Richard knighted me, Kenton bequeathed Saxford to me on the condition I keep it safe from Sutherland. It is his closest property to the border. Even now he tells the tale to anyone who will listen."

"That is quite a . . . uh, Tristan?"

She finally noticed. He'd chosen a horse capable of navigating the rocky incline, but she couldn't know that.

"We're almost to the top, just hang on."

Even beneath the padded gambeson, he could feel her fingers tighten about him. When they finally did reach the crest of the mountain, he bid Hannah to look to her right.

She gasped. "Oh my goodness, look at that!"

He did, though not at the sea.

He really should not have turned around. The urge to feel her lips beneath his own was almost too strong to bear. But he'd made a vow and had never broken it. He would not touch a woman who did not ask for it first. Tristan had spent too many years protecting women to misuse them now.

"I first saw the sea when I was bequeathed Saxford, but I've become partial to living so close to it."

Hannah had not heard him. Or if she had, she gave no indication of it. She was lost to him, if only just a brief moment. When she did look up to meet his gaze, the pain he saw in her eyes nearly made him forget his own vow. He wanted to comfort her but didn't know how except for touch.

"What is it?"

She blinked, a single tear slipping down her face. "I want to go home."

The urge to comfort her peaked, but there was nothing he could do. If her home truly was hundreds of years in the future, she might never see it again. And if she did find a way to return, he'd never see *her* again.

He started the descent in silence.

She was going to die.

Hannah squeezed her eyes shut. She couldn't watch. While she'd climbed Mount Katahdin back home—another adventure imposed on her by Caroline—Maine's highest mountain didn't compare to this. At least she'd been in control, able to put one foot in front of the other. Being this high off the ground on a horse? It wasn't as steep, but if they fell . . .

"You can open your eyes now."

She did and let out a breath. They were at the bottom.

"I need to get down." She'd barely finished the words before Tristan dismounted. After he helped her down, she resisted the urge to fall to the ground and kiss it.

"Please tell me we don't have to do that again."

Tristan led them off the path and into a thicket of woods. He tied the horse to a tree and moved to the bag it carried.

"We do not."

Hannah looked back at the peak behind them. It didn't

even look that steep from here. Back home, it wouldn't even be called a mountain.

"We aren't stopping for long. If you need to . . ."

They looked at each other, Hannah not understanding.

He raised his eyebrows pointedly.

"Oh!" Of course. That she could do. She wandered into the woods to relieve herself, marveling at how much the woods reminded her of home. True, some of the trees were different, but it had the same ambience. She finished, rejoining Tristan once again.

"How are you feeling?"

Since her proclamation about going home, they'd not spoken. Tristan seemed to be deep in thought, and she found herself wondering what he was thinking.

"Better," she said, taking a piece of bread from him. "It just reminded me of Maine."

"What's it like? This 'Maine.'"

Hannah knew he didn't believe her, so the question came as a surprise. "It's also along the coast, the Atlantic Ocean. It's rockier than here, but just as beautiful. Mayport Bay is a typical coastal town."

She took the skin he offered, trying not to dwell on what it was made of. Some sort of animal part, no doubt, but she was content not to know.

"How so?" he asked. Tristan leaned against a tree, taking a bite of some type of dried meat.

"The local industry revolves around the seasons, tourists in the summer months and preparing for them the rest of the year. My parents own . . ."

Owned. Hannah still had a hard time speaking of them in the past tense.

"You don't have to tell me." The sympathetic look in his eyes told her he remembered this part of her story. He'd lost his mother too. He understood.

Suddenly, Tristan was just a regular man again. Not some superhero knight or the lord of a castle that her entire town could fit inside. Just a guy, albeit an extremely good-looking one, who wanted to know more about her life. "They *owned* a flower shop. Bought it from the previous owners when I was four and my sister Caroline was a newborn. It was a terrible time to become business owners, but when it went up for sale . . ."

A sob tried to work its way up her throat. She'd wanted to tell him more about them, but she just couldn't. She wasn't ready. Even with her sisters she had not been ready, knowing she was supposed to be a role model for them. But she just couldn't do it. Not this time.

"Anyway, it came in handy, knowing the flower business," she said, consciously changing the subject.

Tristan pushed away and walked toward her and reached for the waterskin. "What do you mean?"

He drank deeply, his Adam's apple bobbing in a manly display that made her want to kiss his neck. Lord help her.

She took a deep breath as he returned the skin back to the bag. "My degree, an MBA." A blank look settled on his face. "My studies at university. I learned how to run a business and eventually partnered with a former classmate. We started an event planning business in Boston." Of course, he would have no idea what that meant. "We plan things for clients. Weddings, conferences. Um . . . banquets, parties."

She waited for him to process everything from MBA to Boston and conferences. Hannah couldn't help but smile at his expression.

"Are you a steward then? Like Gerard?"

"I suppose. But without a boss . . . a master. We worked for ourselves."

This was clearly a foreign concept to him.

"Everyone has a master. Every lord, an overlord. With the

exception of the king. Now, come. We must make haste." When Tristan mounted and lowered his hand to her, she took it. He lifted her so easily that Hannah actually let out an audible sigh.

You are not attracted to a freaking medieval knight.

Yes, you are. Of course you are.

She stopped arguing with herself and attempted to explain. "We don't have a king. Or a queen. Just a president. But he, and hopefully someday she, can only be elected for eight years at most."

Civics and history were never her favorite classes, but explaining her political system to Tristan forced her to dredge up everything she could remember. After hours of easy conversation as they rode through a changing landscape that became more and more wooded, Hannah was quite impressed with her lessons. It was only when the sun began to set and Tristan announced it was time to make camp that she realized something.

He finally believed her.

ristan set up their camp as he'd done many times before. The most direct route north was as barren as the field of battle had been after Sutherland's defeat. He'd not thought of that day for some time, and telling the story to Hannah had reminded him of why his men prepared to fight back at Saxford. The truce would expire soon, and the vow he'd made to protect Saxford would be tested.

Luckily, Cook had given them provisions since he was not prepared to leave Hannah alone to hunt. He looked up to where she stood at the mouth of the cave. Hands on her hips, head held high, Hannah caught him staring. He didn't look away. And unlike most women, she held his gaze. Tristan walked up the incline toward her.

"You could be the namesake of this cave." He added a log to the fire he'd built, which already cast a glow that reached deep within the entrance of the mountain where they would make their bed this eve.

"Namesake?"

He stopped, not wanting to move too close. Holding her hand earlier had affected him much more than he would have liked, not to mention the sweet torment of feeling her ride behind him.

"It's called Hera's Cave."

"The wife of Zeus."

"And a vengeful woman. Though I'm not sure why 'tis named as such."

Although too many trees stood in the way of the setting sun, a blanket of darkness fell around them, leaving no doubt that the day had, indeed, come to an end. They could have pressed on a bit farther, but judging from the number of times Hannah shifted in the saddle, Tristan could tell she was uncomfortable. For never having ridden a horse before, she'd actually done quite well. A testament to the strength of her long legs.

Legs that had burned a permanent place in his memory.

"So kind of you to compare me to her then," she said, though not kindly.

"I don't compare your temperament to hers," he corrected, not daring to move toward her. "I compare your beauty." Without breaking eye contact, he said, "Some claim Hera to be the most beautiful of all the goddesses. Vengeful, aye, but even more pleasing to the eye than Aphrodite."

She looked at him, unwavering, until the spell was broken by the sound of approaching horses in the distance. His sword was up and at his side before he took a step.

"Wait here."

Tristan made his way through the thicket of trees toward the road.

Reivers. Riding hobbies and carrying long spears, these men were here for one purpose.

"Put down your sword," one of the men called, seeing him. "We've no quarrel with you."

"You are only passing through then?"

Reivers often traveled at night, under the cloak of darkness.

"Aye, lord," the companion said, a nod to Tristan's position more than his clothing. It was the first lesson Kenton had taught him, well before he'd been knighted. *Your bearing reveals more than your background*, he'd often said.

"Aye. Passing through, my lord," the other agreed.

With that, they moved on.

Tristan knew many reivers, and none of those in his acquaintance shied away from a fight. Either these men carried hot goods or they planned on returning later, once Tristan's guard was down, to finish the conversation. Luckily, they had not seen Hannah. He made his way back to find her sitting in front of the fire. He'd set the woolen blanket out earlier, and now he moved to the saddlebags to fetch Cook's meal.

"Is everything okay?"

"All is well," he lied. "Here."

He handed her a pear and then took one for himself. Grabbing a few bits of dried meat to accompany it, he settled on the blanket, choosing the farthest seat from her. If he sat any closer, he'd be tempted to touch her, and he'd already removed all but his hose and undertunic.

"I've no wine to offer you," he said, taking out another skin. "Only ale."

Hannah took it from him and drank deeply. From the look on her face, he guessed they did not have ale in her time.

Though he'd begun to think of her as coming from another time, Tristan was still baffled by the whole thing. Ultimately, he'd had no choice but to believe her story. There was simply no other alternative that made sense given the depth and complexity of her story, her strange appearance on the beach, and her odd belongings.

"No ale in Maine?"

She looked surprised.

"Beer," she said. "We call it beer, and I always thought they were the same. But I guess not. This is hardly recognizable."

They ate in silence, listening to the woods come alive. Having grown up in a town, it had taken Tristan some time to become accustomed to traveling through the woods. The first few times he'd ventured away from home, he had been terrified of the noises that came from the darkness. He was no longer that boy, but that didn't mean other fears did not haunt him.

"So tell me more of it. The future."

While she spoke, Tristan attempted to concentrate on her words. He should be enthralled. After all, she supposedly told him of the fate of his country. Of the world. But all he could think of was running his hands up along the edge of her gown, using her legs as a guide—

"You're not listening," she mumbled. "Typical man."

She seemed to have many comments about the typical behavior of "men." Against his better judgment, he asked her about it. "Are men so terrible then, in your time?"

Hannah took the ale from him, drank again, and frowned. "Some, yes."

And that was all she offered.

Tristan tried again.

"You said women have more 'opportunities' in your time. They are considered equal, allowed to vote—"

"Yeah, well, change is difficult. Moving from your time . . . this time . . . where women are thought of like cattle—"

"Do I treat you that way?"

Hannah's brows drew together. "No, you don't. Why?"

"Why don't I treat you like a cow?"

She laughed, the sound drifting through the night.

"When we first met, on the beach, I thought you were a pompous brute."

"Why?"

"I don't know. I suppose because of your size. And your authoritative manner, ordering everyone around as you do."

"If I order 'everyone around,' it's only because in battle, the men cannot question my words. They must go onto that field knowing I will always do what is best for them, for my people. It's necessary for them to trust me, whatever they may think of the situation."

It had taken some time for Tristan to learn that lesson. His first few years at Saxford had not been easy ones. But he'd earned his people's trust, and he meant to keep it.

She shrugged. "Maybe it's because I dated too many jocks . . . men who play sports and care of little else."

He was curious to know what was considered a sport in her day, but Tristan was much more curious about something else.

"This 'dating' you speak of . . . How many times do you do such a thing if you do not intend to marry these men?"

"Please do not make me explain double standards to you, Tristan."

He had no idea what she meant, so he finished the last of his dried meat and rose to stoke the fire, waiting for her to explain.

"You date as many men as you want, until you find the right one."

Tristan's curiosity got the best of him. "And how many boyfriends have you dated?"

Her chuckle was so unexpected, Tristan frowned. "What have I said?"

"They are two different things. Dating and boyfriends. At least, they can be."

And now he was entirely confused. "In what way?"

"You can date someone, but not exclusively. Which means they are not your boyfriend or girlfriend. That term is reserved for when you only have one."

He wasn't so sure he liked where this was heading. "So you've dated men and had boyfriends too?"

"Yes."

She was laughing. He was not.

When he sat back down, he returned to his spot on the far side of the blanket, ignoring his body's insistence that he sit closer to Hannah.

"How many?" he asked, repeating the question.

"I'll have you know, jealousy is one of my least favorite traits in the men that I date."

He tried to use her same arch tone. "I'll have you know, I care not what traits you like, or do not like, in men. I would just have you answer the question."

"Why?"

"Why what?"

"Why do you care how many men I've dated or how many boyfriends I've had?"

Good question.

"I just want to know what it's like in your time."

"Bullshit," she said, stretching her legs out in front of her. The traveling gown was simple, thinner than the others and quite becoming on her. Thank God he had won his argument with her this morning. She'd thought to wear those "shorts" again, but he'd refused, knowing he could not bear it for any length of time.

"An epithet I haven't heard before," he said, laughing.

"Yet you knew it was one." She indulged him. "I don't know how many men I've dated, but I've had three serious boyfriends."

He changed his mind . . . he didn't want to know.

"The last one was the most serious, until he dumped me for his ex."

"Pardon?"

"Ex-girlfriend."

He was going to comment on the fact that this foolish man had chosen another woman, until he realized—

"You said most women in your time are not virgins when they wed."

Hannah brought her knees up to her chest and hugged them. Whether she was trying to get comfortable or deliberately tormenting him, Tristan couldn't be sure. But when she pressed her knees to her chest, the swell of her bosom called to him. His hands ached to touch her there. Everywhere.

"Aye," she said, chuckling, apparently at her own attempt to sound like him.

"So you are not—"

Her smile disappeared. "That is an awfully personal question, Tristan. Do people in this time usually speak so openly about such topics?"

"I did not mean to offend you."

He could see only her outline, courtesy of the fire and the faint light from a hazy moon.

"You did not offend me."

He was glad for it. "If there is no such thing as nobility, inheritance—"

"Some women, and men, are virgins when they marry. I didn't mean to give you the wrong impression of my time. It's just that many are not."

"That was not my question."

"I am not."

The jolt of lust hit him, strangled him, refused to let go. This meant nothing. Certainly it did not mean—

Hannah wanted to ask him something. Her face was

always so expressive. If she could hide her emotions, she certainly did not try.

"I know you are not shy, Hannah. Ask."

He was not usually so impertinent. Not with strange women, at least.

"Did the women in the stewhouse . . . that is . . ."

She stopped.

"They taught me everything I know," Tristan said sincerely. "And not only in the arts of love. When I was old enough, big enough, to protect them, my mother no longer needed to spend coin on a guard. By then I'd been training under Kenton, growing stronger every day." He smiled. "Some of the women noticed."

He hadn't talked about the past for years. He wasn't ashamed of it, but it did not serve him well to remind others of who he'd been.

"I see."

She didn't. Not really. He'd love nothing more than to show her, and the look on her face told him she'd love it too. Normally, he would welcome such a look in a woman he desired. But not tonight. Not with her. She was neither common nor a widow, and she was leaving on the morrow.

He moved to stand—to retreat from the fire, from her— but she stood at the same time. She took one step toward him, two. Three.

He could have reached for her she stood so close. Kissed her despite the risk. But he wouldn't.

"So this is also something very different about our times," she said, her voice slightly louder than a whisper.

"What is that?" he asked, despite himself.

Hannah smiled. A slow, sensual, beautiful smile.

"In my time, by now, you would have kissed me."

8

*C*hrist.

Tristan had never backed down from a challenge, and he sure as hell was not going to start tonight.

As Tristan reached for her, Hannah leaned in toward him. He had only a brief glimpse at her face, the lips he so desperately wanted to feel against his own, and then he was clasping her cheeks in his hands.

He touched his lips to hers, and she immediately opened to him.

Her kiss was no innocent virgin's touch; nor was it the measured caress of a courtesan. As her tongue reached out to meet his own, Tristan took advantage. He tried to be gentle, but her response wouldn't allow it. She hungrily took what he offered and gave the same in return. His rough hands moved from her face to the back of her head, grabbing her silky hair with both fists.

When she groaned, he pressed harder, moved faster, desperate to taste her. No kiss had inflamed him so quickly, and when she pulled back, he silently thanked every saint at once.

That would not have ended well. It would already be difficult to let her go—no need to make it harder.

"I take it back."

Tristan could not help but smile. She looked exactly as she should, a woman properly kissed. He wouldn't be surprised if he looked much the same. That kiss had taken him more by surprise than the day King Richard had turned an armorer's apprentice into a lord with one deft stroke.

"Our times are not so different." Hannah licked her lips one last time before stepping away from him.

Aye, Hannah, they are. No woman here has made me feel that way before.

Apparently they were going to act as if the kiss had not happened.

Very well.

He leaned down to grab a log from the pile. Either they had been lucky to find dry wood in the cave, or they'd unknowingly commandeered someone else's lodging. It was getting late, but he did not discount that the reivers may return.

"Are they not so different?" he finally asked. With an adequate fire, he turned his attention to the bedrolls.

"That was . . ."

He paused, looking up at his beautiful traveler, waiting for her response.

"Like a regular kiss."

It had been anything but.

She must have read the look on his face, because she hastened to say, "I mean . . . not regular. Actually, not at all. But maybe I thought it would be different somehow."

Once he'd prepared the makeshift beds, Tristan sat on his. Having changed his position, he could no longer see the valley below them, but he'd exchanged it for a much more pleasant view. She stood in the exact spot where they'd kissed.

"Do you know what I mean?"

"No," he said. "I do not."

Though he should be insulted by her casual declaration that his kiss was quite ordinary, Tristan found himself amused instead.

"Perhaps you should explain." He had a feeling she could not, but he looked forward to her attempt.

"It was regular," she said, "in that it was the same kind of kiss a man would . . ."

His eyes narrowed.

"Never mind."

She lifted her gown, moved toward the bags, and pulled something out.

"I'm going to change."

He didn't realize at first what she meant, but when Tristan saw what she carried in her arms, he snapped, "No, you are not."

She appeared as if she would like nothing better than to throttle him. But he paid her no mind. She was not going to wear those "shorts" again.

"Yes," she said turning, "I am."

He stood, raising his brows at the stream of colorful language she spouted as he followed her—words like "ass" and "brute."

"If anyone sees you—"

Hannah spun around. "Anyone? There is no one here to see me. Only you. I don't understand why you're so opposed to my clothing."

Surely she jested.

"No respectable woman—"

"Don't you dare."

He ignored her flash of anger. "This is not Maine, Hannah. Do you not understand? It is dangerous out here."

"And who exactly am I in danger from?" She turned to look toward the road and then back at him. "I see no one here except for you. And I am not from fourteenth-century England. I already told you, this is what we wear. And it's perfectly acceptable. Bare legs are not an invitation. Anyway"—she tugged at the low neckline of her gown —"how is this any better? Talk about a double standard."

Tristan wasn't sure how to answer, so he did not.

"I get it. I need to play by your rules. That's why I've worn Joan's ridiculous dresses for more than twenty-four hours now. But there is no one else here, and I refuse to sleep in this thing."

"Your shift—"

"Is much more decent than these." She lifted up the shorts and hoodie in her hands. "But you know what? This isn't about clothes. It's about the fact that you don't believe me. If you did—"

"I do," he said.

"But not totally. And you know what? If I were in your shoes, I'd think I was crazy too. But I'm not. I'm just a New England girl who is terrified the waterfall my sisters and I jumped into yesterday will have no answers for me."

Tristan reached for her, but Hannah pulled away.

"You're scared."

"Damn right I'm scared. I'm more than scared, I'm terrified. What if I never see my sisters again, Tristan? What if I can't get back?"

It was the question that had hung between them since the start of their journey—or at least since Tristan had begun to believe her. When he reached for her this time, she did not resist, and he smoothed her hair back away from her face as she began to cry. It was not the first time he'd comforted a woman, but never before had he been this eager to do so.

Hannah was unlike anyone he'd ever met, rightly so given her circumstances, and she faced impossibly high stakes. If for some reason they did not find the answers she needed tomorrow, she would be alone in a world that was not her own.

He pulled her more tightly against him.

"If you can't get back," he said, struggling to find the right words, "you will stay with me."

IF YOU CAN'T GET BACK, you will stay with me.

She didn't know what to say to that. Maybe he really meant it, or maybe he'd only made the offer because he felt sorry for her.

How embarrassing.

Hannah couldn't remember a time when she'd cried in a man's arms. Literally. The wrenching sadness seemed to have come out of nowhere. She'd actually been feeling much better this evening, talking with Tristan and teasing him.

Kissing him.

How could she have said it was like a "regular" kiss? When his lips had touched hers, she'd felt . . . consumed. Utterly and completely filled with a longing to be near him, to memorize every inch of him for when she was back home. She'd wanted nothing more than to get closer to him, as close as possible, and that had scared the spit out of her. Scared her enough to pull away. To lash out. To distance herself.

Good job on that front.

But her self-protection strategy had utterly failed, because she now stood wrapped in this virtual stranger's arms so tightly that anyone who saw them would swear they'd known each other for—maybe more than one day?

She sniffled, and though she'd stopped crying, Hannah did not move. Whenever she cried, her face became a blotchy mess. It had nothing to do with how good his arms felt around her. She resisted the urge to move her hands just a few inches to see if those arms were as muscled as she thought they might be. The man would think her out of her mind. Crying one minute, putting moves on him the next.

"Are you feeling better?"

She sighed, aware he was going to get a good look at her face at some point. She pulled back, wiping away the last remnants of her ridiculous outburst.

"Much," she lied.

He didn't let go of her, and Hannah really didn't want him to.

"I don't cry," she announced.

Tristan raised his brows.

"Not like that."

He still looked skeptical.

"I'm the strong one," she announced. It was true. And somehow, even though her sisters weren't here with her, it mattered now more than ever.

Tristan leaned down and placed a soft kiss on the tip of her nose.

"Of course, my lady."

He stepped back and bowed.

"Your wardrobe room awaits," he said, pointing to a thicket of trees just next to them.

Hannah hugged the clothes against her chest.

"I am no lady," she said. "At least, not in the way you mean it."

"And how is that?"

And just like that, it was over. They'd so quickly reverted

back to their easy banter that Hannah could almost forget the kiss and the moment of weakness she'd spent in his arms.

Almost.

"Nobility," she said.

"Of course, there is no such thing in your time."

"Not in America at least."

In the end she decided not to comment on what he'd said about her staying. She didn't want it to matter. If it did, that meant they would discover nothing at the falls, and that was simply unacceptable. As she'd done since waking up on that beach, Hannah pushed thoughts of her sisters away. She concentrated instead on getting out of her constricting gown. Luckily Joan had thought of the trip she would be taking, and aside from the snag she left in the ties at her side, it was easier to manage than she'd feared.

Judging from the maid's scandalized expression when she'd helped her prepare for the journey, it was highly unusual for an unattached man and woman to travel alone together. Luckily, Hannah couldn't care less about her reputation since she would not be going back to Saxford.

And if you don't find a way home?

She pushed the negative talk away since such thoughts were completely useless. She *would* see her sisters again. She would go home.

What she would not do was see Tristan again after tomorrow. A thought she refused to dwell on since there was nothing she could do to change that.

She'd just folded the borrowed garments as neatly as possible into a pile, placing the traveling gown on top, when the sound of twigs cracking turned her attention to where she'd left Tristan.

He appeared from nowhere, sword in hand.

His eyes widened—she was buck naked—and then he was gone.

What the hell was that?

Hannah could hear him running in the opposite direction, toward the road. She got dressed as quickly as humanly possible and gathered up her belongings. Now what? Go back to their camp or follow him?

The distant sound of a man's scream made the decision for her. Hannah ran toward their shelter as fast as her legs would carry her. She tossed the bag with her things out of the way and threw the pile of clothes on top. The cave was more like an overhang, but Hannah slid as far back as she could. Heart hammering against her chest, she watched little bits of ash float above the fire and dance away. She couldn't hear a thing, and for the first time since yesterday, she thought of what would happen to her without Tristan. She'd felt perfectly safe, even when he'd told her how dangerous it was here, but only because of him. The man was a certifiable knight, a warrior if she'd ever seen one.

And yet he was not infallible . . . what if something happened to him? What if he was already dead?

Just like he had earlier, Tristan appeared out of nowhere.

She jumped up from her spot and ran to him. "You're alive!"

Hannah nearly threw her arms around him but came to her senses just in time.

Tristan looked her up and down, his gaze resting on her legs, which were getting cold despite the fact that it was July. She pulled her hoodie tighter to fend off the sudden chill.

"You're dressed."

When she met his eyes, the pupils dilated with desire, Hannah's pulse raced. He wanted her, and she very much wanted him. She looked away, down to the sword he carried in his hand, and gasped.

"There's blood all over that."

While he stood there appraising her as calm as could be,

his massive sword—a broadsword, according to what one of the tour guides had told them—dripped blood as he held it next to him. This was not the shiny sword that might be displayed at a museum. It was worn, well-used, and freaking bloody.

The same panic that had made her shed every stitch of clothing that time she'd cut her foot took over. She reached out and turned him, inspecting everywhere. No blood. He played along and allowed her to turn him back around.

"You're not hurt."

"Nay," he said, "but I do need to clean this."

"What happened?

His lips pursed just slightly and his eyes . . . he could hypnotize someone with that look.

"I heard a noise and came to check on you—"

"I know that," she said, impatient to learn the rest of it. "And then?"

"And then I encountered the same two men who had come through earlier. Whether they'd planned all along to come back or—"

"The blood, Tristan?" How could he stand there talking to her so calmly when something catastrophic had clearly happened?

"And then one of them attacked me. Which leads me to believe—"

"Tristan! You're sure you're okay?"

The look he gave her in response to that question turned her on more than anything else ever had in her entire life-time. It was so assured, so damn confident—as if he were incapable of losing a fight, and the mere suggestion of it was so insulting that he appeared unable, or unwilling, to answer.

"Is *he* okay?" she asked instead, dreading the answer.

"Does it matter?"

Her mouth dropped open. Had he just killed a man?

He moved away from her then, pulling out his sword and walking toward the foot of the cave.

She turned and watched in fascination as he pulled a cloth from the saddlebag and began to wipe the blood away. Was she really watching this?

"It matters to me," she said at last.

Finished, he tossed the cloth into the fire and placed his sword on the ground next to one of the bedrolls in the mouth of the cave.

"No," he said finally. "I did not kill him."

He sat and nodded toward the empty bedroll next to him. "We'll be leaving at first light."

Oh my God. For real? He was just going to go to sleep after that?

"Tristan," she said, attempting to remain calm. "What happened?"

She made her way toward him slowly, cautiously. Not that she was afraid of him. It was just . . . she'd only seen two men fight, really fight, once in her life. During her senior year of college, some jerk catcalled her right in front of her boyfriend in a nightclub. Without saying a word, her boyfriend hauled back and punched the guy in the face, the sound one she could still remember. They were promptly tossed out of the bar.

Sure, she hadn't seen anything happen this time, but she'd seen the outcome on his sword. She sat and waited, staring at him expectantly.

"A shoulder wound," Tristan said. "It was enough of a warning, and at least I'll be able to sleep now."

"What do you mean?"

"They knew we were here, so I planned to stay awake to be sure they didn't return. Most likely they'd only planned to steal the horse—"

"But how did you hear them? I couldn't hear a sound.

Well, I barely could anyway, even when you were down there."

Hannah pulled a blanket over her legs. Though it was a scratchy wool one, at least it would keep her warm.

For the first time since he returned, Tristan smiled. And while his bedroom eyes had been something to contend with, this was much, much worse.

"I have many skills, my lady, that you're not yet aware of."

9

"*I*s this familiar?" Tristan asked.

Hannah looked around, avoiding *him*. As expected, she had not slept much the night before, kept awake by worry about her sisters, and what fitful slumber she'd managed was filled with dreams of a certain handsome medieval knight.

Tristan was no longer the man who had found her lying on a beach, but the one who had kissed her, who had made his desire for her known even as she tried to deny her own feelings. Every glance, every touch—no matter how innocent or casual—was an invitation. A challenge.

And every bounce that brought her hips to meet his backside reminded her not only of her desire but of the need to arrive at Leannan Falls and sort out this mess.

"Maybe?" she said, wishing she'd paid more attention that day. She'd spent the ride to the falls chatting with her sisters about leaving Scotland and fending off their pleas for her to return home. She certainly had not been studying the landscape, which had all looked pretty much the same. "It's hard to tell. The last time I was here, there were roads leading up to the trailhead. Houses and—"

"We've avoided the main roads and stayed away from villages, especially around here. I am not sure, but we may already be on Clan Sutherland land."

Hannah could feel Tristan tense. From what he'd told her, she knew how dangerous that would be. And yet he'd chosen to accompany her anyway.

"Tristan, thank you for—"

Tristan turned, putting his finger to his lips. He pointed ahead of them and to the right. A small stone cottage with a thatched roof came into view. It appeared to be abandoned, but clearly Tristan was taking no chances. He only spoke once they were well beyond hearing distance, and even then his caution made her a bit nervous.

"If the borderlands are truly as dangerous as you say, why would anyone live here? That was no Saxford Castle back there, its defenses—"

"Do not exist. Which is likely why it was abandoned."

They rode along, the day as cloudy and gloomy as the previous one had been bright and sunny. She refused to think of omens, but it made her anxious nonetheless.

"But even Saxford . . ." Tristan shifted, forcing Hannah to tighten her arms around his waist. "Nowhere is truly safe along the border."

He was silent for so long, Hannah thought Tristan may have forgotten her question or decided not to answer it. When he did speak, the deep baritone of his voice touched her soul.

"It is more than a location, more than a home. Borderers are a resilient people whose loyalty is pure and whole. We would not live anywhere else, unless forced to do so, as I suspect happened back there."

He could have been talking about Mayport Bay, and she could hear her sisters' voices in Tristan's words. They had such a happy childhood in a town that many came to visit year after year, some tourists making it their permanent home. They'd never understood her decision to move to Boston.

"I left my home," she found herself saying as if it were a confession.

Tristan lifted his head, and she heard it then. A waterfall in the distance. Her pulse pounded in her veins as she looked around for familiar landmarks.

"Why?" he asked, wresting her attention away from their surroundings.

She could hear Caroline asking that same question. No matter how many times she tried to explain, neither of her sisters completely understood.

Maybe Hannah didn't quite understand herself.

"It's a small town. I always knew I'd leave someday. Or at least after I got into college, I knew—"

"University?"

"Aye," she smiled to herself, realizing college and graduate school meant nothing to him. Yet for a while, it had been her entire world. The day she received her acceptance letter to Yale was one of the happiest of her life. "After growing up around my parents' shop, I knew I wanted to start my own business. I didn't know what I wanted to do at first, but Mayport Bay offered few opportunities. Boston, on the other hand . . ."

Hannah loved everything about Boston. Moving there had been the right move for her career.

"But you miss your home?"

"Before my parents . . ." She sighed. "I did miss it. But there's nothing there for me now."

"Other than your sisters," Tristan said.

Did he sense her regret? Spending these last weeks with her sisters had only reminded her how much she missed them.

The sound of the falls was getting louder now, and when they finally turned a corner and the source came into view, Hannah could hardy sit still.

"This is it!"

She wanted to jump off the horse, and would have if Tristan had not reached back and stayed her.

"Easy." He held her in place and navigated through the dense woods toward the clearing beneath the falls. He finally dismounted and helped her down from the horse.

As soon as she landed on her feet, Hannah ran through the remaining trees. Just beyond the tree line, a wall of rocks framed the water tumbling from above. It looked, unbelievably, just as it had the last time she was here. Frantic now, Hannah rushed down to the spot where she and her sisters had stood before deciding to jump. The dry rock outcropping afforded a spectacular view of the entire falls.

She felt Tristan fall in behind her as she scanned the majestic sight before her. According to the innkeeper who had suggested the day trip, some said Leannan Falls was Scotland's best-kept secret. As ethereal as the more well-known faerie pools on Isle of Skye but tucked away in a wooded and otherwise secluded area, the falls attracted more serious climbers and cliff jumpers than it did casual tourists.

But her relief quickly faded. "Nothing," she said, turning to Tristan. "I don't see anything out of the ordinary. Do you?" she asked, aware of the desperation creeping into her voice.

The last time Hannah had stood here, she'd been laughing and joking with her sisters, feet firmly planted in the twenty-first century. She wasn't sure what she'd expected, but she'd hoped to find something, anything to indicate what had happened here—and how she could reverse it. Like maybe some fantasy-type portal back to the future . . . or her sisters. Had she really let herself believe they'd be waiting for her?

Before Tristan could respond, Hannah ran to a spot closer to the lower falls. Still nothing.

She shook her head, unable to think.

"No," she said. "No, no."

Hannah looked back up and knew what she had to do. She started climbing.

"Hannah, where are you going?"

She ascended the same path Caroline had pointed out just two days ago. This was the path "non-jumpers" used, leading to an outcropping above a particularly deep spot in the pool beneath.

"Hannah?"

She should say goodbye in case it worked. Thank him for bringing her here. Ignoring the pang in her chest at the thought of never seeing Tristan again, she looked down to where her future, and past, awaited. Most importantly, to where her sisters awaited.

"I have to know," she said, positioning herself in the very same spot she'd jumped from before. Fear bubbled up in her gut as she looked down on the pool so far beneath her, but she'd made the jump once and could do it again.

Relief flooded through Hannah when she saw Tristan approaching, navigating the wet rocks to the spot where she stood. He held out his hand, and she took it without hesitation.

"You intend to jump?"

Hannah wanted to do more than squeeze his hand back. She wanted to kiss him, to feel his arms around her once more. But it wouldn't do them any good. She didn't belong here.

"I don't have any choice," she said.

Tristan peered over the falls. The distance wasn't dangerous. The more experienced jumpers, the daredevils, jumped from the higher perch above them.

He nodded, letting go of her hand. "You're scared."

"Damn right," she said. Delaying the inevitable was actually making it worse . . . both her fear and her reluctance to leave him. She leaned up, placed a kiss on Tristan's cheek, and turned back to the falls. "Thank you for everything," she said. Then she gathered her courage and stepped off the ledge before she clung to him and never let go.

And for the second time that week, Hannah fell through the air and plunged into the frigid waters of Leannan Falls.

———

SHE WAS GONE.

Tristan had seen the look on her face as they rode here. Hannah had been to this place before, but not like this—the Leannan Falls she'd visited had featured "roads and highways" that would not exist for years. If he had harbored any remaining doubts before, he didn't now. She truly had come from another time, and now it appeared she'd gone back to that place.

Or not.

When her head bobbed out of the water, Tristan didn't think. He tossed aside his sword and jumped in after her. When the cold water pulled him under, he swam to the surface.

There!

She did not appear to be in any danger—of course she could swim, she'd never indicated otherwise. He'd simply panicked, something Tristan had never done before. But when he caught sight of Hannah's expression, a look of complete terror, he was glad he'd jumped in.

"Come here," he said, pulling her toward him.

He treaded water with Hannah beside him. For a moment he just held her, and then he guided her to the rocky bank, his feet slipping as he scrambled out of the water.

"Hannah?"

She stared straight ahead, shoulders slumped. He sat next to her and waited for her to speak. Oddly, he had not expected her to emerge from the falls. And in that moment when he'd thought she had somehow gone back to her own time . . .

Tristan shook his head, trying to clear his thoughts.

"We have to find them," she finally said. "We have to find my sisters."

Hannah's bright eyes and easy smile were gone, her inner fire snuffed out.

"We will find them," he said, though he had no idea if such a thing were possible. Were her sisters here or back in Hannah's time?

"What if we don't?"

Hannah stood, nearly falling and steadying only when Tristan reached his arm out for her.

"They aren't here. It didn't work. If jumping from the falls doesn't take me back . . ."

Tristan did the only thing he could think of to calm her down.

He kissed her.

Maybe it was an excuse . . . maybe he simply needed to reassure himself that she hadn't left. Either way, he savored the soft touch of their lips, and when it was no longer enough, he deepened the kiss. Holding her face in his hands, the sound of the falls behind them, Tristan tried to tell her that she would not be abandoned. He didn't know if they would find her sisters or if Hannah would ever be able to go back to her time, but he would be there with her to find out.

When she pulled back and relaxed against him, he wrapped her up in his arms, marveling at how perfectly she fit against his chest. Part of him wanted to stay like this for longer—maybe forever—but he was soaking wet, cold, and not in the least bit comfortable about being on Sutherland land. Tristan allowed himself to hold her for just a moment longer. Finally, reluctantly, he let go.

"We need to change," he said, taking her hand.

"And then?"

"And then we go home."

Hannah pulled her hand away. "Home? I have no home, Tristan. My home is . . ." She pointed to the falls. "There. Somewhere on the other side. I can't go back to Saxford with you. I need to find my sisters."

The woman he'd met was back.

Good.

"Will you wander through the woods, looking for them? What is your plan, Hannah?"

"Plan? My plan was to find . . . something here that would help me understand. But the only thing here is a goddamn waterfall and—"

"You cannot stay here."

Eyes narrowed, she stared at him as if he were the enemy.

"Come back to Saxford. I will send men back north to question the locals. They will search from here to Edinburgh—"

"I will go with them."

"No, you will not. Have you not been listening, Hannah? What will it take for you to understand how dangerous it is here? Even during times of peace."

"But your men won't know my sisters by sight. And what will I do at Saxford? Twiddle my thumbs until they return?"

Tristan didn't know what twiddling was, and if he said what he was thinking, he risked making Hannah even angrier. But he couldn't help himself, so he smiled anyway.

"I may have an idea about that . . ."

"My lady?"

Hannah opened her eyes, blinking against the light that peeked through the shuttered window of her chamber. She should be grateful to even have a window, since many areas of the castle did not.

Instead, she wanted nothing more than to go back to bed.

Two days had passed since they'd returned from Leannan Falls. She kept hoping to wake up and realize this was all just a dream. But it wasn't, and if her sisters were indeed marooned in the past with her, there was no sign of them.

"Aye, Joan, I'm getting up."

Waking. That would have been the preferable thing to say. Every time Hannah opened her mouth, it seemed she spoke a word or phrase that was foreign to the fourteenth century. Her presence was already a circus sideshow, and she didn't need to bring additional attention to herself. But she simply couldn't help it.

From the way she ate to the words she spoke, everything about her seemed strange to Tristan's people. He had told them she was a widow, but apparently that had done little to sway them. Hannah wasn't stupid. There were not many women here, and all of them shot her scornful looks that told her how inappropriate it was for her to be here, alone and unchaperoned.

As for the men . . . they either seemed to hold her in suspicion or want to sleep with her. She'd had to swat away more than one wayward hand.

So much for the chivalric code.

But it was Gerard, Tristan's steward, who appeared to trust her the least. He eyed her with suspicion, as if she would take his job. Or perhaps she only imagined it knowing his duties most closely aligned to her skill set. Gerard was one of the first people Tristan had met when he began to train under Lord Kenton. Perhaps it was simply their close bond that made the man so leery of her.

Back home, his attitude would have mattered. Hannah liked to be liked. But here she was an outsider. An unwelcome guest. An interloper who wanted nothing more than to leave and never come back. She did not belong, and so the usual rules did not apply.

And yet . . . at least one person seemed happy to have her here.

Tristan had been an utter gentleman since their trip to the falls. True to his promise, he'd sent his men on a mission that she hoped, prayed, would find some answers. In the meantime, she waited. And tried her best to acclimate to life at Saxford Castle.

Hannah had spaced out while Joan helped her dress up in her newest doll-like outfit—a silken chemise and cranberry velvet gown. When she snapped back to attention, Joan was saying, "With Kenton comin', Cook is as irritable as ever."

"Kenton?"

"Aye, my lady. Lord Kenton is coming to Saxford."

Tristan hadn't mentioned his mentor would be visiting.

Although she'd hardly seen him, so maybe she shouldn't be surprised.

"Why does that make Cook irritable?"

Joan's eyes widened. "You've not met 'im yet?"

Hannah shook her head. "No. And I don't believe I care to if he's that irritable."

"Aye, you'd do well to avoid him."

Hannah smiled. "Duly noted." *Dammit.* "I meant to say, very well. Thank you."

Joan wasn't fooled. But for some reason, she didn't seem to hold Hannah's strangeness against her.

"May I ask you something, Joan?"

Hannah turned as Joan began to work on her hair. She'd tried to tell the woman she was perfectly capable of brushing her own hair, but she'd have none of it. Apparently she had been assigned to Hannah's care, and from what she could tell, it was a job that was taken seriously, even if the "lady" was of questionable moral standards.

"Of course, my lady."

She would never get used to that. Though Tristan had explained it was an address of respect more than one that denoted a title, which, of course, she didn't have, it rang false to her ears.

"Why are you so kind to me?"

The question seemed to surprise the older woman.

"I mean, everyone else treats me like a leper."

Joan shrugged. "They do not know you, my lady."

"But you hardly know me either."

Finished, the maid spun her around and smiled at her own handiwork.

"Aye, but I know enough. I know you are kind, and that you make my lord smile."

Joan picked up Hannah's discarded nightdress, a satin chemise, and shooed her from the room.

"Go now, my lord is waitin' on you."

"Tristan?"

Joan frowned. Apparently no one else called him that. But she'd be damned if she called him anything but. It was the only semblance of normalcy she had around here.

"Aye, my lady. He's in the hall."

Odd. Since their return, she usually only saw him at supper, and she'd begun to think he was avoiding her. Hannah had told herself it was fine. The last thing she needed was an attachment to a man who lived in a different century.

So why was she so excited to hear he'd sent for her?

TRISTAN HAD NEVER ACTED like such a coward in his life. Each night he dreamed of Hannah, and each morning he awoke from a deep slumber with the feel of her lips on his own. But his feelings for her scared him, and so he'd walked away from them—and her. It helped that there were plenty of preparations that had required his attention. Now that his men were ready and his allies on alert, he needed only to await the raids, and likely attacks, that would be forthcoming once the truce with Sutherland ended.

His thoughts had lingered more and more on Hannah, and he'd realized it had been a mistake to stay away. And so he'd devised a plan to make it up to her.

As she walked into the great hall now, he made his way toward her, trying to ignore the fact that every man present was fixated on her.

"Good morn, my lady," he said.

"Tris . . . my lord."

He knew they were being watched. Counted on it in fact.

"Tristan," he said, his voice firm. Though it would invite

further speculation, the familiarity would also ensure Hannah was not treated poorly. At least overtly. Tristan was aware how Hannah had been treated thus far at Saxford. He'd attempted to mitigate the worst of it, but it wasn't enough. He, more than anyone, was aware of the stigma that came with even the merest perception of impropriety. Hannah had arrived under dubious circumstances, unchaperoned, and with nothing but the force of her personality. His people had taken notice.

"I have a proposal, my lady." He would only call her Hannah in private. That she was given leave to use his given name, but that he did not do so in return, was also a message of respect.

Hannah appeared just as she had since that day at the falls. Sad. Defeated. Unlike the woman he'd met that first day on the beach. And not at all the same as the one who had kissed him at their camp.

Which is why this day was not likely the best of his ideas. But necessary nonetheless.

"I'd like to take you to the village," he said. "You've met so few . . ." He almost said, *of us*, but he had to give care to how he spoke to Hannah around others. No one, not even Gerard, whom he trusted with his life, could know the truth. It was simply too fantastical. Too dangerous.

"You've met so few people here."

"Why?"

Indeed. A good question that warranted an answer. The truth would not do. Instead, he said, "I thought it might be . . . of interest."

She didn't trust him. Why would she in light of how he'd abandoned her? But as she cocked her head to the side, Tristan found himself praying she agreed.

"Very well," she said.

Tristan smiled.

"Good. Come."

He strode from the hall at a brisk pace, assuming Hannah would follow. It was only when he began to descend the stairs to the ground floor that he looked behind him. Where was she?

"Right now?" she said, rounding the corner. He was pleased to see the hint of a smile on her face. "Will we not break our fast first?"

He laughed. "At least you have the right of it today. When I first heard the term breakfast—"

"And don't forget lunch."

He shook his head as he continued down the steps. "It truly is as if we speak different languages at times."

"Honestly," she called from above him. "It doesn't much matter what you call it. I'm famished."

He assumed that meant some form of hunger.

"I've had Cook prepare food for us," he said as they exited the main keep. He pointed to their mounts. "There."

Hannah stopped. "I cannot ride myself. You know I do not—"

"We will take it slow," he said, thanking the groom who had chosen the perfect horse for Hannah. "Her name is Arwen."

For someone who had no experience with horses, Hannah had done well on their journey—enough so that she was likely ready to ride herself. At least he hoped she was ready. He couldn't bear the torture of having her body cradled so close to his.

"She was a gift from Kenton," he said. "To my mother."

Hannah's hand froze on the Spanish mare's shoulder.

"Your . . ."

"Mother," he repeated. Nodding to the groom, who helped Hannah mount, Tristan climbed atop his horse.

"That's it," he said. "Sit up straight, just as you did with me. Hold the reins only as firmly as needed."

Hannah glanced over at him, and Tristan could not hold his laughter at her expression.

"Well done," he said, despite her glare. And it was true— her posture was perfect. "Now squeeze with your heels and tell her to walk."

Hannah did exactly as he instructed. "Keep your chin up and look forward."

As he rode alongside her, instructing her on how to guide the horse's movement—"Press your calf gently on the right." "And now the left." "Stay with her."—an audience began to form. Someone shouted a word of encouragement while another clapped as she began to get the hang of the horse's movements.

Once she had mastered a few basics, they rode toward the gatehouse, cheers echoing in their ears. If his people thought it odd a lady did not know how to ride, they would know better than to comment on it in his hearing.

"Now squeeze your thighs."

Tristan inhaled. Best not to visualize that. "See? She is slowing down."

"To stop completely, pull back on the reins," he said as they rode through another gate along the North Mere. Saxford was surrounded by the North Sea on one side and three meres on the others. Additional gatehouses guarded the small areas between each of the lakes.

"Don't pull back too quickly," he said. "Easy . . . there you go."

She looked at him as if she'd been granted a boon. "I'm doing it. I'm really doing it!"

Indeed, she was. She looked magnificent atop Arwen's back, her eyes sparkling and her back straight.

"Remember," he said when Arwen reared a bit. "Every

movement should be slow, deliberate." If his voice sounded different, it was because his imagination had conjured an image of her riding *him*. Tristan looked away, concentrating on the landscape in front of them. "Are you hungry?" he asked, remembering that she'd asked him about food.

"No . . . *nay*," she said. "I'm too excited to eat."

A comfortable silence fell between them as they rode side by side, enjoying the warm weather. They would not reach the village until midmorning, but he waited until Hannah looked comfortable enough to talk.

"She likes you." He nodded to Arwen.

"I like her too," she said, glancing at him. "I'd love to know more about her previous owner."

The look in her eyes told him she meant every word. She wanted to hear more about his mother, and for the first time in a long while, Tristan felt compelled to talk about her.

"She died two years ago," he said. "Just after she agreed to move here with me."

"I'm sorry, Tristan."

"Her life was a difficult one," he said. "I would have enjoyed giving her the security Saxford could offer."

"She didn't want to come earlier?" Hannah asked, navigating Arwen as if she were an expert horsewoman. The road to the nearest village was flat, a perfect first ride for her.

"The Swan was the only establishment of its kind not under the control of the church," he said. "She worried what would become of it if she left. My mother selected the women carefully; all were examined to ensure their humors were balanced before working for her. But she took care to treat them well, something other stewhouses were not always reputed to do."

"She sounds like a caring, ambitious woman."

Her tone lacked any hint of derision.

"Aye, she was . . . perfect."

Maybe not to the world, but to him.

"She died in her sleep. The ladies said a pain in her arm and vomiting sent her to an early bed. And, it seems, an early grave. She should have been at Saxford. With me."

Hannah grew quiet suddenly, and Tristan ventured to ask her the same question she'd asked him.

"Will you speak of your parents?"

When Arwen suddenly reared, Tristan shouted, "Keep your weight forward. Don't pull on the reins."

She did as instructed, and the horse quickly calmed. "That's it," he said, grateful he'd chosen a horse with such an easy temperament. "She sensed your unease. You may have pulled back or tightened your legs without realizing you'd done so."

Hannah took a deep breath and finally looked over at him. "I believe I did just that."

Neither of them needed to say it aloud—the subject of her parents had clearly upset her. Tristan didn't bring it up again, instead finding ways to distract her. They spoke at greater length of the differences between their times, though much of what she said was difficult to believe.

Time passed like water with Hannah, and before Tristan knew it, they'd reached the gentle ridge leading in to the village. What would she think of it?

"Slow down," he said as they reached the top. "And look."

He watched as Hannah looked down and gasped.

---

*H*annah had visited "medieval" villages while in Scotland, full of Tudor-style homes and quaint shops, and this looked nothing like them. This was a real medieval village, not some re-creation or throwback to an earlier time.

Frankly, it terrified her.

She should be used to the shock by now, but every time she was confronted with new evidence of the time jump, Hannah's brain went into overdrive. She couldn't speak . . . could hardly breathe.

Holy shit, she was sitting astride a horse, next to a knight, above a medieval village filled with huts. She was living in the fourteenth century.

"Hannah?"

"I'm fine."

"Clearly you are not," Tristan said next to her.

"I will be."

"Come," he said, spurring his mount forward.

"The most fertile fields are that way," he said, pointing

beyond the village. "The marshlands we rode through are good for grazing, but not much else."

Not surprising. They'd passed a windmill, but other than that, there'd been no signs of life.

They rode down a slight decline, Hannah trying not to grip the reins too tightly.

"Though small, Saxford Village serves the people well."

As they approached the village, Tristan's face lit up. "There is the church," he said, pointing to the only building that had an actual roof rather than some clay-straw hybrid. "And that building, the forge. Our smith is quite skilled, but he's had some help."

Tristan was clearly proud of the skills that had gotten him noticed by Lord Kenton. Rightly so.

"Are a smith and an armorer the same thing?"

Tristan led her to a building not far from the forge. He dismounted, helped her to do the same, and then tied their horses to a wooden post.

"Nay, they are not."

He didn't elaborate. "Wait here."

A stable. She couldn't tell from her earlier angle, but as Hannah moved around the building, the sounds and smells from within revealed its purpose. She turned toward the center of the village and watched children playing with a ball that looked like it was made of string. They paid her no mind, but the same could not be said for the adults.

Hannah had always assumed peasants, if that was what these people were, would not be well-dressed. In movies, they always looked like their clothes were about to fall off their bodies. But there were a few young women in the crowd, and the only real difference between their dresses and hers was their gowns' fabric and lack of adornments. Otherwise, they were styled similarly.

She felt Tristan behind her before he spoke. Awareness of him washed over her, sending a shiver down her spine. Hannah had been so nervous and excited to ride all on her own, she'd nearly forgotten her attraction to him.

Nearly, but not quite.

There was no use denying it. Not that it mattered much since this was only a temporary home for her. Hannah chuckled aloud at the thought of returning to Boston pregnant, fielding questions about the baby's father.

"What is it?" he asked, his voice so close to her ear it sent another shiver through her.

"Nothing," she said, turning. "Where to?"

"Afternoon, my lord."

"Albert," Tristan said to a short, bearded man headed in the opposite direction. They walked past the forge, away from the playing children, and Tristan exchanged greetings with several more of the townspeople.

"This isn't at all what I expected," Hannah said, turning to see the women still staring at her.

"No?"

Tristan was looking at her the way he always did. Boldly and straight into her eyes.

"No." She pointed off into the distance to a structure she could not identify from here. "What is that?"

"The mill," he said as they approached a two-story building. While the lower roof was made of stone, the upper layer was some sort of clay that seemed to have been mixed with hay. A sign depicted a fox and a goose, though it gave no other indication of what was inside.

"What is it?" she asked as he opened the door.

"A tavern," he said. "The Fox and Goose."

She turned back to give him a look that said, *Seriously? That was the name of the tavern?* Apparently he was. The name was as clever as the one Allie had given to the family cat when they were kids. She and Caroline teased their little sister mercilessly for naming her "Kitty." But to be fair, they had gone along with it.

When she stepped inside, Hannah smiled. For a moment, she felt like she was back home. At least the old-style taverns in Boston had gotten something right. Wood everywhere and a stone fireplace, which adorned one wall, made it distinctly British-looking. Darker than it should be given that it was daytime, it was also much busier than she expected. Shouldn't the men be working in the field?

"So many people here," she whispered.

"During high season, it might be unusual for such a crowd this time of the day. But during low season?" He shrugged. "And it's nearly time for dinner," he said.

"You mean lunch," Hannah teased.

"My lord." A serving girl winked at him as she walked by.

"She *literally* winked at you." Hannah sat opposite Tristan at a small table near the back of the hall.

"I won't ask what that means," he said, raising his hand in the air.

A moment later, another woman, this one much older, approached them.

"My lord?" she said. "Ale and a meal?"

"Aye," Tristan said, his smile making the serving maid flush. She couldn't be a year younger than fifty, but his appeal was ageless.

"It means," she whispered as Tristan seemed to nod and smile at every single person in the room, "that she likes you."

He turned his attention to her. "Does it now?"

Was he really that dense? "People don't just go around winking at each other willy-nilly. And certainly not at the lord, unless . . ." She stopped talking. "Oh."

Of course, she couldn't care less if they'd already slept together. Hannah only glanced back at the girl . . . nay, she was very much a woman . . . out of curiosity. When she shifted her attention back to the table, Tristan was looking at her.

She didn't like that look. God help her, she could not resist that look.

"Aye?" she asked. Hannah loved that word. If she ever made it back home, she was taking it with her. She smiled. Everyone would think she had gone batshit crazy.

"We are at the tavern. Now what do we do?"

"What do you mean, now—"

The cad.

Tristan sat back and crossed his arms, waiting for her to understand what he'd done. She couldn't resist the smile that spread across her face.

"A date," she said, though it wasn't quite a question. "You think we're on a date?"

Hannah's pulse pounded as the day took on a whole new meaning. So he'd intended this from the start? Why?

Why else do people date, Hannah? Don't be thick.

"Are we not?"

She could have objected to the arrangement, told him that two people have to agree to be on a date in order for it to qualify as such. Or that plopping her in the heart of a medieval freakin' village was not a date, it was the basis for a movie. But what came out of her mouth was far removed from either of those things.

"Aye, Tristan. I suppose we are."

God, she hoped she wouldn't regret this.

Tristan couldn't remember ever enjoying himself this much.

The look on Hannah's face when she surmised they were on a "date," as she called it, was surpassed only by the outrageous impressions of him and his men she'd done after drinking three mugs of ale. She had so mastered Gerard's direct, gruff manner that if he closed his eyes, Tristan could imagine his marshal was sitting at the Fox and Goose with him. He had been surprised when she expressed concern that Gerard, and others, may not look kindly toward her.

Aside from that brief moment, their conversation remained lighthearted. And enjoyable. His urge to consummate their desire grew, but he would not do so lest she did find a way back to her time. There were ways, of course, to prevent a babe. But Tristan had seen too many of The Swan's women use them and become mothers anyway. But could they not find enjoyment in other ways?

"I think it best we leave before you have difficulty riding back," he said after Hannah finished her fourth mug of ale.

"A whole new notion of drunk driving," she muttered. Hannah often said things that made no sense to him, and he'd learned when to ignore her strange comments.

They left, walking back to the stable in another companionable silence. Hannah smiled at everyone, and to his delight, they smiled back. If she stayed, they would warm to her, accept her. Tristan was sure of it.

"I'll retrieve the horses," he said, disappearing into the stable. She nodded her assent, but when he emerged with their mounts, she was gone.

"Hannah?" he called.

Tying the horses to an iron ring beside the stable, Tristan began walking, telling himself she was nearby. Could she have gone back home? But how? There were no falls here . . .

and her last jump had only landed her in a pool of cold water—

"Tristan, in here." Relief nearly brought him to his knees when she waved to him from the door of the blacksmith's forge and then slipped back inside.

"I met George," she said, her eyes bright, as he followed her inside. "He is quite skilled."

The blacksmith did not look up, but Tristan saw the slight smile the old man tried to hide. Hunched over the anvil, he pounded away at the orange steel he was working.

"What is he making?" Hannah asked over the noise.

Tristan took a step toward George and watched as he pounded away.

"A broadsword," he said as the old man looked up. Beads of sweat dripped from his withered brow. "Where is your new apprentice?"

George frowned. "Quit, he did. Said he missed his ma."

He had not seen the smithy in too many moons, and he looked to have aged quite a bit. Tristan rolled up his sleeves, took an apron from the wall, and found a pair of gloves.

"What in the name of—"

"Move over," he said, knowing if it didn't come as an order, the other man would hammer all evening, tired or not.

When he reached out, George gave him the piece of iron and hammer. He went to work before it could cool and only looked up once to find Hannah watching him intently. By the time he finished, the piece of iron had begun to take shape. It would need two, perhaps three more days before it was finished.

"I'll be back tomorrow," he said to George, handing him the iron.

"My lord, you—"

"Will finish the weapon now that I've started it."

George grinned like a squire. "Thank you, my lord."

Then, turning to Hannah, he said, "And thank you for bringing 'im here, my lady."

Tristan reached out, without thinking, and offered Hannah his hand. As soon as they emerged, he realized what he'd done and released it.

"That was amazing," she said.

"It was just a sword," he said, though he didn't quite mean it. Every piece was unique, and it had felt good to be back inside the forge. "What made you go in there?"

They approached the horses, and Tristan assisted Hannah, careful not to allow his touch to linger, and then mounted himself. They began the ride back.

"I heard the hammering," she shrugged. "And wanted to see what it was that you did exactly. Though I still don't see the difference between the two positions." Pink rose on her smooth cheeks. "In terms of being a blacksmith and an armorer, I mean."

He could say something bawdy but decided against it.

"I made only armor. George forges swords, daggers, even jewelry."

"But that was a sword, and you knew how to—"

"An armorer can make weapons, and a blacksmith can make armor."

Hannah made a face. "Perhaps some things in our times are just too different to comprehend."

Tristan thought about that for a time, and likely Hannah did the same. He had not intended to stay so long in the village, but as he watched the sun dip in the sky, Tristan suddenly had an idea. Something he thought Hannah would enjoy. If they were going to make it, they would have to hurry.

"Do you think you're ready to trot?"

Hannah shook her head.

"Good, follow me."

"Tristan!"

Sometimes the best way to learn was just to do. And when he turned back to see her cantering along as easily as if she'd been raised riding, he smiled. He navigated off the main road and slowed down as trees began to appear. If he was correct . . .

"This way," he shouted back. This was it. Tristan dismounted and turned to help Hannah do the same. After tying up both horses, he took her hand for the second time that day and led her to a break in the trees.

Just in time.

They watched, hand in hand, as the sun set in a magical display of reds, oranges, and pinks. It would make a beautiful memory, Tristan thought—for her, hopefully, and for him. Years after she went back to her own time, he would remember her easy laughter and strange ideas. He would remember this.

But she isn't gone just yet.

And he was no monk.

Pulling her toward him with their joined hands, Tristan brought his lips down on hers and waited until Hannah opened herself completely. Though he plundered her mouth, his tongue tussling with hers in a dance common to both of their times, it wasn't enough.

Groaning, he pulled her closer until he could feel her luscious breasts pressing against him. He kissed her harder, then trailed a line of kisses down to her jaw, her neck. Hannah responded by lifting her head to give him better access. He trailed his lips down, lower and lower, until the valley he sought was within reach. He slowed then, giving deference to the sacred place he was about to enter.

With one hand, he pushed the material of her gown aside, and with the other, he gripped the small of her back. Though he could not reach her nipple, the soft, warm mound under his lips gave him enough of a taste to know he wanted more.

Much more.

He stood and looked down at her partially exposed breast, her swollen lips, and her bemused expression.

"Do you want me to stop?"

Hannah swallowed. "No . . . nay. I'd rather you not."

1 2

$\mathcal{H}$annah had spent the better part of a week imagining what this exact moment would feel like. She'd had an inkling of it that night at camp, but this was much more than an inkling. It was a full-fledged assault on her senses, and she didn't care what century he was from.

She didn't know what he was asking for beyond permission to continue, but it hardly mattered. Well, maybe it mattered a bit.

"We can't have sex, of course." She frowned. "Or make love, or whatever you call it."

"Of course."

He reached for her and, clasping his hands around both buttocks, lifted her up against him. She clenched with pleasure when his hardness pressed against her.

"What are you—"

Tristan put her down at the base of a nearby tree and leaned her against it.

"—doing?"

He didn't answer.

Instead, Tristan leaned toward her until his lips were

nearly touching hers. "I am doing what I should have done that first night we slept together."

He kissed the corner of her mouth.

"We didn't . . . sleep together," she managed.

"Oh aye, but we did."

He kissed her cheek, her jaw, her neck.

"In my time," she said, gripping his surcoat with both hands. "Sleeping together means the same thing as having sex."

"Is that so?"

Hannah closed her eyes as a moan slipped from her lips. He'd moved on to her ear. After kissing that, he buried his face in her neck and breathed in so deeply that Hannah was sure he could feel her heartbeat against his chest.

"What are you doing now?" she asked.

In answer, he grabbed a fistful of her gown at its hem and pulled it upward. Somehow, with only one hand, he managed to hike both layers up to her waist and expose her legs to the early nighttime air.

He lifted his head and winked. "In my time, we don't talk so much. We feel instead."

With that, he opened his palm wide against her leg and held it there. Then, lowering his head, he opened her mouth for a kiss that demanded her response, which she happily gave. Hannah met every thrust of his tongue with her own as his palm pressed and squeezed against her inner thigh, moving slowly but steadily upward.

Hannah had no choice but to respond. She pushed up against him, meeting each bit of pressure with her own until she couldn't take it any longer. As if reading her thoughts, he pulled his hand back and lifted her gown for better access, letting his fingers rest on the very precipice of her fulfillment.

"You can't stop there."

If he wanted a challenge, then she would offer one. And her words did seem to embolden him . . . One moment, she was pressing her hips forward, and the next she could barely stand. He'd slipped his fingers inside her and knew exactly what to do with them. Thank goodness for the tree behind her.

"How . . . ," she managed.

He kissed her neck, darting his tongue out each time his fingers surged inside her, the two motions mimicking each other.

Ever since she'd washed up on the shore of Saxford Castle, Hannah had gone to bed each night imagining this. Wondering how it would be with Tristan. Wondering how he would be different.

She didn't have to wonder any longer.

There was no comparison.

When he brought his mouth back to hers, Hannah kissed him hungrily, all other thoughts banished by the expert maneuvers of one very skilled Englishman. She pulled her mouth away as the pressure built, the need to scream almost inescapable.

"Tristan."

Hannah's eyes popped open just as the wave crested. Every muscle in her body tensed, save one, and when Tristan smiled, she came completely undone. Heart hammering in her chest, she attempted to catch her breath.

He pulled away from her finally, fixing her gown and continuing to smile like a man who knew he'd given the ultimate pleasure. God, he was divine. Hannah looked down, and though his surcoat partially concealed his arousal, she was pretty sure he was as hard as a rock.

"You can't ride like that."

Had she ever blurted out a more ridiculous thing in her life?

"I've managed before," he said, leaning down to place a quick, and unbelievably sweet, kiss on her nose. "We need to leave before it grows too dark. I'm impressed by your riding skills, but . . ."

But she wasn't quite ready to navigate Arwen at night. Well . . . she was not ready to navigate Tristan either, so it was just as well.

"What do you mean you've managed before?" she asked as they walked back to their horses. Hannah wasn't a hundred percent steady on her feet yet.

He patted her horse with care and then lifted Hannah up with the same gentle ease as he'd done many times before. How could a hardened warrior have such gentle hands?

She shuddered.

Tristan mounted and turned back to her.

"All the way to Scotland . . . and back," he said, his meaning clear as he glanced at the back of his horse, where she had sat on their journey.

Hannah took a long, deep, steadying breath and squeezed her legs, signaling Arwen to walk. It didn't work. No amount of deep breathing would erase that memory or quell the very scary thought that had bubbled up.

She was falling for Sir Tristan, Lord of Saxford.

And falling hard.

By ALL THE SAINTS, that should not have happened.

Tristan paced back and forth in his chamber, knowing it was past time for supper and not caring. He'd been with enough women to know something astonishing had happened today. Something that defied reason. He'd known, of course, she was different. After all, Hannah came from a very different time and place than this. A different world almost. But he had not expected her passion would bring him to the point of losing control for the first time since he'd begun to enjoy the company of ladies.

When he'd watched her earlier today, felt her beneath his fingertips, one thought had taken root in his soul.

He wanted her to stay.

The relief he'd felt when she'd surfaced in the pool at the foot of the falls . . . he'd told himself at the time it was simply because she was safe. But after today, Tristan would be a fool to deny that if the men he'd sent to gather information came back with a way for Hannah to go home, he would be devastated.

A knock on the door disturbed his thoughts.

"Come in," he called.

"My lord?" Gerard entered the chamber and closed the door behind him.

Tristan pursed his lips in annoyance. "Tristan," he amended. "Why you insist on the formality—"

"It is necessary."

"No, it is not. When we first came to Saxford—"

"We were young and foolish," Gerard finished. "And you were desperate for legitimacy."

He never did hide his true feelings, which was usually one of the things Tristan liked best about him.

"And I have it," Tristan said.

Gerard shrugged. "Aye, you do. And the title is well-earned which is the reason I use it. But I didn't come here to quibble over your title. Your lady is belowstairs already—"

Tristan did not like his friend's tone. "You will not disparage her, Gerard."

"I did no such thing."

He studied his friend's expression and realized he may have come to that conclusion erroneously.

"I only meant to say she appears different this eve. More relaxed. But she is still clearly waiting for you to appear."

Tristan had known Gerard long enough to suspect his friend had not just come here to discuss Hannah's demeanor. His next words confirmed it.

"What are you doing, Tristan?"

"I don't know." He had always been honest with Gerard.

"Can you at least tell me where she came from? I was there on the beach that day. And I still—"

"I cannot tell you."

He wouldn't expand upon his lie, not with Gerard.

"Look at you," Gerard said, interrupting his thoughts. "I've never seen you like this before, so . . . distracted."

Likely because he'd never felt this way before.

"If I could tell anyone, it would be you. And maybe someday . . ." Tristan ignored the pang in his chest at the idea of revealing everything to Gerard once Hannah was gone. "Just know, for now, she is likely not staying long. And as I've said, she is no spy. Just a woman without a place in the world, for now."

That Gerard should understand. They'd both been in that position themselves.

His friend nodded once, solemnly, and added, "And one who is waiting for you below."

Tristan left his thoughts of the future behind and followed his steward through the winding corridors and down to the great hall. Stopping in the threshold, he watched as Hannah sat laughing with the cupbearer who poured her favorite wine. He'd meant to ask the laundress where she had managed to find Hannah so many gowns.

If Hannah stayed, Joan would make a fine lady's maid.

She is not staying.

Except Gerard was right—Hannah *did* look different this eve. With a quick glance around the hall, he also noticed not as many watched her with suspicion. He left the steward, who refused to dine at the high table no matter how many times Tristan had attempted to persuade him otherwise, and joined Hannah.

"Apologies for my tardiness, my lady," he said, sitting beside her.

Typically the lightest meal of the day, dinner normally consisted of soup and possibly one other course. But Hannah had told him the opposite was true for her—she was accustomed to a dinner more akin to their supper. And so he'd asked Cook for an additional course each night.

"You look lovely this eve," he said.

An understatement so vast it might as well be a lie.

Hannah was more than lovely. She was exquisite. Perfect, really.

"Why thank you, kind sir," she said with a smile, mimicking his speech.

As they ate, they spoke of their day. The village. The weather. Her first horse-riding expedition. Anything but what had happened between them that afternoon. But he was suddenly feeling adventurous.

"So would you consider it a successful"—he lowered his voice, the word foreign to all but Hannah—"date?"

His reward was a sly smile that told him she had accepted his challenge.

"I would say so, aye." But then she cocked her head as if reconsidering. "In a way."

Hannah took a sip of vegetable soup, her pink tongue darting out to test it first. He immediately hardened, which reminded him of the uncomfortable ride back earlier that evening.

"And why do you say so?"

Gerard watched them, brows furrowed. He did not need

to ask what worried the man. His fascination with Hannah had come at the worst possible time.

Kenton's visit. The end of the treaty. An impending attack.

The future was full of challenges, but she likely wouldn't be here. Today, she was next to him. And he did not wish to squander the time they had left.

"There's much I still don't know about you," she said, surprising him.

He raised his brows, inviting her to continue.

"Such as how easily I can bring you to the same place as you brought me to today."

Tristan choked on his ale. He would have spat it out had he taken a fuller sip.

"For a moment," he said, "I thought you meant—"

"Aye? What did you think?" she asked sweetly, her eyes sparkling with mischief.

Every time she said the word "aye," it reminded him of her attempts to acclimate. And while she was doing it well, to say Hannah Sutton blended into his world . . .

"I think," he whispered back. "It will be a very interesting evening indeed."

Before she could respond, a commotion at the entrance commanded her attention.

13

*H*annah strained her neck to see what was happening as Tristan stood and made his way toward a group of men, newcomers, entering the hall.

"Kenton," Tristan exclaimed loudly enough for everyone to hear. "I didn't expect you until tomorrow."

So this was the famous Lord Kenton.

Hannah couldn't hear the man's response from across the hall, but when Tristan and his mentor turned toward her a few moments later, she had no doubt whom they were discussing. Gerard led the other men away while Tristan and his mentor made their way toward her.

Kenton was not at all what she had expected. Even if Tristan had not called him an old man, he spoke of him with such respect and deference she would have expected him to be much older. He was no more than fifty with not a gray hair to be found. His close-shaven but full beard, as black as the hair on his head, made him look as fierce as Tristan had upon their first meeting.

Kenton's expression didn't help matters.

It wasn't his lack of a smile that unnerved her. He met her

eyes as he approached the dais, and his serious gaze, coupled with his unwavering eye contact, would have made a younger Hannah shift in her seat. As it was, she'd dealt with celebrity clients and CEOs who could, and had, made their interns cry. Dealing with him would take finesse, something she had in spades.

She stood.

The social norms of this period eluded her still, but Hannah had been taught never to shake hands from a seated position. She hoped the same was true of bowing, since she would be required to honor Kenton's elevated station—the only useful tidbit of information she'd absorbed from her tours of Scottish castles was that the motions of bowing and curtseying had been basically the same before the seventeenth century.

"Kenton, I would like you to meet Lady Hannah Sutton."

"Good evening to you, my lord," she said with a bow.

"This is the man I told you was passably good at wielding a sword," Tristan said with a smirk.

In fact, Tristan had told her Kenton was an excellent swordsman—in his prime, he'd claimed more than his share of honors in tournaments throughout England.

"The pleasure is mine," he said, nodding to her seat. Hannah sat back down and watched as Kenton took a seat on the other side of Tristan. Below them, Gerard had led the others to their seats, and the servants were already coming around with soup for the newcomers.

The first time she won the New England Award of Excellence in Business, Hannah had felt as she did now—distinctly out of place. She hadn't allowed her nerves to rattle her then, and she certainly would not do so now.

Once he was settled, the older man leaned forward to meet her eyes once again. "Tristan says you are visiting from overseas, my lady?"

They really needed a better cover story if she was going to stay here for any length of time. Though she fully expected, somehow, to get swept back to her time—or at least to her sisters—she had no idea what the timeline would be.

"Aye, my lord," she said, hoping Tristan hadn't left the details of the lie to discretion.

"How long were you in Venice?"

Hannah nearly spat out her wine. It took every ounce of self-control not to laugh at Tristan, who was the picture of innocence at the moment.

Hopefully Kenton was not as versed in Italian as his former ward.

"Not long," she said. "When my parents died, I vowed to become a student of the world. You see, my father always wanted to travel and never had the opportunity," she said, sticking to the truth as much as possible. "In their honor, I have been moving from place to place. Lord Saxford was kind enough to allow me to stay here as I mourn the loss of Kitty."

Now both men appeared confused. "My lady's maid," she clarified.

Lord forgive her for lying. And for not thinking of a better name for her nonexistent maid. Her cat had indeed died, so there was that.

"Ahh."

"How goes Kenton Castle?" Tristan interjected. "And Berwick?"

Hannah pasted a smile on her face, grateful to Tristan for redirecting Kenton's attention.

"Restless. The end of the truce and the lack of interest from the wardens thanks to the growing power of the noble magnates, a distraction for the king, guarantees a renewed volatility courtesy of Clan Sutherland."

"I made a vow that day that I intended to keep," Tristan answered.

That day . . . the one where Kenton had granted him Saxford in exchange for his protection of one of the most contentious regions along the border. She supposed it was a good deal, but after what she'd seen in the forge, maybe Tristan would have been just as happy as an armorer.

He would certainly have been safer.

As the men discussed Tristan's preparation for the expiration of the truce, Hannah's thoughts drifted far away. The talk of Sutherland had reminded her of a weekend trip she'd taken in college. She and three of her friends had visited West Virginia, the home state of one of the girls. They'd gone to a festival celebrating the end of the rivalry between the Hatfields and McCoys. One of the famous families' surviving relatives—Hannah couldn't remember from which side— spoke just before the lead band played in the evening. He said that the reconciliation of their two families was proof that anyone could reach an accord.

Or something like that.

Was a lasting peace truly out of the question? She would have to tell the story to Tristan.

He looked worried. A week ago she would have missed the signs—the way he bit the inside of his cheeks and ground his teeth so subtly it was hardly noticeable. How safe were they here at Saxford? Would she be in danger if she remained here much longer? Could she truly leave never knowing Tristan's fate? Or having to look it up as a part of distant history?

"Lady Hannah," Kenton said, breaking her out of her reverie. "How long do you plan to stay in England?"

Did the man read minds?

As Tristan watched her, waiting for an answer, Hannah

struggled with what to say. She'd planned to say "not long," but the intensity of Tristan's gaze changed her mind.

"I'm still not sure," she said, keenly aware her modern-sounding language made her stick out like a sore thumb. Kenton gave her a strange look, but there was nothing she could do to take back what she'd already said. All she could do was put forth her most proper manners.

For Tristan's sake.

"I will say, the circumstances by which I find myself here are second only to the tale of how Lord Saxford came to be here himself."

Kenton set down his soup spoon, glancing at Tristan with fatherly pride.

"He told you of the battle, I presume? He was too modest, I am sure."

Tristan rolled his eyes and directed his attention toward his meal.

"In all my days I'd never seen a man fight like that. I was only glad the king recognized his bravery and service."

"Enough talk of battle and bravery," Tristan said. "Lady Hannah has heard of nothing else since she arrived."

Though it was true, Hannah did not tire of it. She liked to hear of Tristan's successes. Certainly, his stories were a far cry from life in Boston or Mayport Bay.

"Aye," Kenton said. "Let us discuss something more appropriate for your guest." He raised his mug to her, drank deeply, and planted it back on the table. "My niece is staying with us for a time," he said. "Her needlework is quite fine. I trust you enjoy embroidery, Lady Hannah?"

She stared at the man in horror. Though her grand-mother *had* made her mother's wedding gown by hand, Grandma's talent with a needle had not passed down through the generations. Not to Hannah, at least.

"An instrument, then?"

Hannah shot a look at Tristan, who appeared to catch on to her dismay.

"Lady Hannah finds . . . out-of-door pursuits more to her liking," Tristan said.

This ought to be good.

"Indeed?" Kenton was trying his best to feign polite interest. "Hawking, then?"

Uh, not exactly. She shot Tristan another, more desperate, look.

"Walks in the woods," he blurted. "And riding."

When Kenton looked back at her, Hannah was the epitome of good grace. She smiled and nodded, trying hard not to laugh.

Their conversation shifted back to the conflict with Sutherland, thankfully, and she allowed herself to drift again.

Embroidery? Music? Hawking?

Was that what a life of a lady entailed?

Of course it did. This was not the twenty-first century, and if women had a place of importance here, it was the exception and not the rule. Even the allure of staying with Tristan couldn't compensate for that dreadful fact.

Staying with Tristan? Impossible.

Still, there was no denying the idea had crossed her mind. What if she discovered Caroline and Allie had come through time as well? Would they want to stay or go back if such a thing were even possible?

Don't be ridiculous. Even on the off chance they did want to stay, she could not. She'd spent the past several years building a successful business, and the very idea of subjecting herself to these fourteenth-century notions of womanhood . . . nay, it was a silly idea.

She could never, ever stay here. Not in a million years.

"DON'T GO BACK."

Tristan stood beside her at the falls, knowing she was prepared to jump. Knowing, somehow, that it would work this time.

"Tristan, I . . . I must." With that, she took a step toward the edge of the falls, and he knew he was about to lose her, he knew . . .

"Tristan."

This time, his name was in Gerard's voice, and the image of Hannah on the precipice of the falls faded from his vision. A dream, then. But hadn't his mother always told him dreams told the truth?

After four days with them, Kenton had left that afternoon. They'd spent most of the night before continuing their discussion of the Sutherland threat, and after a long day of training, Tristan must have fallen asleep. He couldn't remember the last time he'd slept during the day.

"How long did I sleep?"

Gerard crossed his arms. "You missed supper," he said, "which I thought was most unusual."

Damn.

He had seen little of Hannah these last few days. After the first night of Kenton's visit, she had avoided taking an active part in their talk at dinner. He could tell she'd been frustrated with the older man's questions. Coupled with the fact that the men he'd sent to scout for her sisters—or any information about Leannan Falls—were due back any day, she was not herself.

In the meantime, her easy manner had accomplished the impossible. It seemed Hannah found an unlikely friend. She and Cook, known for his surliness, had apparently been inseparable these last few days. Tristan was curious about that rumor and anxious to mitigate the damage Kenton had done.

He loved the man like a father, but he could be difficult at times. Tristan's mother had always commented on the lord's high-handedness, however grateful she'd been for his role in Tristan's life.

"As long as you are well," Gerard said, "I will take my leave. Good eve, my lord."

His steward grinned, knowing how much the title annoyed him, especially when used in private. He was well past caring about appearance, and anyone who knew Tristan's history knew better than to expect conventionality to reign at Saxford. It was why his people had accepted Hannah so quickly.

A few moments later, a servant arrived with a wooden tray. Gerard had evidently ordered the meal, but Tristan wasn't hungry.

For food at least.

He'd thought about going to Hannah nearly every single night, only to remember all the reasons he should not.

But Tristan no longer cared about convention or propriety or all the differences that stood between them.

Hannah was in his blood. The memory of their day in the village would not leave him. He awoke each morning feeling the phantom pleasure of her body pressed against his. When she smiled at anyone but him, Tristan wanted to pull her into his arms and make her forget anyone else existed.

His will had been tested every day and night, and tonight it failed him.

He needed to see her.

Now.

14

Hannah closed the door behind Joan and turned back toward her bedchamber. She'd asked for a fire even though it was high summer. Summers in Maine could be cool, but a constant chill lingered in the castle—one of many things Hannah struggled to adjust to.

The list was extensive.

And yet . . . these past few days she had settled into more of a routine than she'd thought possible. Kenton, who'd inadvertently reminded her of how out of place she was in the fourteenth century, had reminded her of all the reasons why she could never stay here. Despite . . . well . . . him.

But she'd decided to make herself useful for the rest of her time in Saxford, and since Tristan had been closeted away with Kenton and his marshal, she'd decided to start with the next most important person in the household.

Cook, known by no other name, was everything she'd expected. Burly, gruff, and completely uninterested in her meddling, he'd kicked her out of the kitchen no less than three times before she made any headway.

Eventually she wore him down the same way she would any difficult client. By being helpful. Ignoring the strange looks she attracted, she donned an apron and refused to leave the kitchen. And while Cook continued to present his unapologetic rough manners, Hannah ignored his blustering. She'd actually elicited a smile from him later that first day. And hugs from no less than two kitchen maids, who'd thanked her for "such a miracle."

Since then she had showed him new dishes, at least ones that were possible with the ingredients at hand. Although she did not cater events herself, Hannah knew enough about them to understand how large amounts of food could be made, and served, efficiently. Cook had been much more open to her suggestions as the days wore on, and she found herself enjoying their time together.

Walking toward the hearth and reaching out her hands to warm them, Hannah sighed in contentment. It was actually kind of cozy with the fire.

She almost hated the thought of going back to the bright lamps and fluorescent lighting of her office. Her room, like the rest of the castle, was lit by the soft, warm glow of candles and wall torches, which gave it all a very . . . medieval feel.

The knock at the door couldn't have startled her more if it had been a tractor trailer barreling through her room. She'd never been so on edge back home. Not before the accident anyway.

Assuming it was Joan, Hannah pulled the door open without hesitation. "Did you forget—"

"Oh," she said, shocked to see Tristan filling the doorway. As many times as she'd thought of going to him, or imagined him appearing at her door, she should have been more prepared. Instead, she simply stared. Allie would certainly not call her a "paragon of politeness" if she could see her mouth agape just now. Something about him made her much more expressive, even outspoken, than normal.

When his gaze dropped to take in the white silk chemise Joan had chosen for her, Hannah's heart thudded in her chest.

"May I come in?"

It was not a good idea. In fact, it was a terrible one. But there was no chance in hell she would say no.

"Aye."

Hannah stepped aside and Tristan entered the room, which immediately felt half as big, and closed the door behind him.

"Nice of you to bring two," she said, pointing to the sole goblet he held.

"Gerard had it sent to me when I missed the meal. Care to share?"

She didn't answer and instead watched as Tristan strode to the small table against the wall.

Hannah could not help staring at Tristan's backside as he poured the wine. The thin material of his hose did little to hide a very shapely—

She jerked her head up when Tristan cleared his throat. A younger Hannah would have been quite embarrassed to have been caught staring. Now she felt invigorated.

He handed her the wine, ever a gentleman, and Hannah took a sip, attempting to slow her racing pulse as their fingers touched. Normally she hated sweet wine, but even the sweetest of Saxford's vintages would be considered dry by modern standards. Though different than what she was used to, it was not altogether bad.

Hannah handed the wine back to him.

"I've not slept during the day," he said, his voice deep and low, "as far back as I can remember. After staying up with

Kenton . . ." He stopped and took another sip of wine. "I was sorry to have missed a moment alone with you."

When he handed back the goblet this time, Hannah took a healthier swig of it.

"He cares for you," she said. To her mind, it was the one quality that recommended Kenton.

"But you do not care for him."

Not usually one to be self-conscious, Hannah neverthe-less found herself squirming under his gaze. She walked over to one of the two chairs in front of the fire and sat.

Tristan sat across from her, watching her and waiting, apparently, for her to continue.

"In my time, he would be called a male chauvinist."

Seeing his confused expression, she attempted to explain. "A man who believes females are inferior."

Tristan appeared to consider her words. "He does believe as much," he finally said. "Though I do not."

"I know." If he had thought so, Hannah would have never, not even briefly, allowed herself to imagine what a life at Saxford would be like.

Not that he'd asked her to stay. Or that she could ever, ever consider such a thing, not knowing if her sisters were safe.

"But there are many men like Kenton."

"In my day as well. Women have more rights in the future, but still . . ." She shrugged. "My mother warned me before college that it was still a man's world in many ways, as if I needed the warning."

"You have spent your life trying to prove the opposite."

Hannah froze.

She had to think about what Tristan had just said. She replayed the words in her mind. Some part of her wanted to deny it, but she took a sip of wine instead.

"The biggest fight I ever had with my sister, the middle one—"

"Allie?"

Hannah smiled, pleased he had remembered.

"Allison, but yes, we call her Allie. Mostly because I wasn't able to say her full name when she was born. Anyway, when Mom and Dad died, we assumed Caroline would take over their shop. When she didn't, Allie suggested I move back home. She wanted me to sell my own business and take it on myself. 'I would do it,' she said, 'but what does a nurse know about running a business?' And she would have. Putting that 'for sale' sign up was difficult for her. For all of us." She paused for a moment, remembering the conversation. She'd been so angry with Allie for implying she should give up her career as if it were nothing. That she should just give up and go home after all the endless hours she'd poured into it.

"She accused me of much the same," she finally said. "She knew I loved my business but wished I could bring it to Maine, where my clients would be much less demanding. But also less . . ." Hannah stopped. "It doesn't matter."

"You told Kenton your father had always wanted to travel."

He knew she wanted to change the topic. God bless him, the man was astute.

"There was truth to what you said to him," he observed.

Hannah prayed for strength. She was going to need it.

"His family was originally from Scotland. He'd dreamed of a vacation to his 'homeland' for his entire life. But their business made it difficult for them to get away, and there was just never a good time." She took a deep breath. "So when they were killed in a car accident, we decided to come here for them."

Hannah stared at her hand, which now had a white-knuckled grip on the goblet. "We took some of the money from the sale of the shop and agreed to come here on the one-year anniversary of the accident. We all needed it, but Caroline did the most. We worried about her . . ."

Hannah trailed off.

She sensed him before she saw him. The great hulk of an English knight lifted her chin ever so gently, until their eyes met.

"I am sorry about your parents."

Not as sorry as I am.

"We will find your sisters, Hannah. I promise you. We will not stop looking."

When he leaned forward, Hannah welcomed his touch. She wanted it . . . nay, needed it. The soft brush of his lips was meant to soothe. To comfort, not caress. But that small taste of him was not enough.

She leaned forward and invited another, which he happily accommodated. This time, his kiss was more insistent. When she opened for him, Tristan's tongue swept inside as if it belonged there.

Perhaps it did.

He took the goblet from her hand as they both stood. What had begun as something tender and sweet was quickly turning into much, much more.

When he broke away and placed the goblet on the table, Tristan did not come back to her immediately.

"I cannot stay away," he said, as if he were confessing some grave sin.

"Then don't."

Such an easy solution. She'd spent days thinking of all the reasons they should stay away from each other, but now she couldn't think of a single one.

He looked like he was going to argue with her, but instead Tristan strode toward her and slammed his mouth against hers in a kiss that was as passionate and possessive as the first one had been gentle. Within seconds their tongues tangled as they spiraled down a dangerous slope that Hannah knew she would be powerless to stop.

Before she could form a coherent thought, Tristan swept her up into his arms and carried her to the bed. He didn't break contact as he lowered her and continued the delicious assault. She clamored to get his shirt off, eager to see how accurate her imagination had been. Complying, Tristan yanked it off over his head.

Her mouth dropped open.

Sitting beside her was a perfect specimen, the epitome of manliness. Unlike the muscle-heads who lifted next to her in the gym, Tristan's muscles were formed more naturally. Years of training had brought them out in all the right places without looking . . . artificial.

She couldn't help it. Hannah reached up and laid her hand on his upper arm. When the muscles beneath her fingers twitched, she let her fingers continue their exploration until his groan alerted her that her time was up.

"Your turn," he said, reaching down to the fabric beneath her knee. His hand glided up ever so slowly, moving up toward her inner thigh where no barrier stood in his way. The combination of his rough hand and the smooth silk of her chemise elicited an involuntary shudder.

"One of many, I hope."

She'd have answered, but his fingers found her at that precise moment. Hannah lifted her knees to give him the access he sought.

"Is this type of caress common in your time?" he asked, his deep voice only adding to his appeal.

He entered and withdrew, teased and tormented as if he'd been trained by the author of the *Kama Sutra* himself.

Hannah nodded.

As he brought her to the brink of climax literally seconds later, he asked, "And this?"

She was undone, unable to answer. Hannah closed her eyes and allowed herself the pleasure of a sweet release and the aftermath. She didn't need to open her eyes to know Tristan had lowered himself beside her.

When she did open them, his head was propped up on his hand, his perfect, naked torso splayed out in front of her, begging to be touched.

And so she complied.

"So these are what real muscles look like?"

Tristan raised his brows. "Real muscles?"

Not in the mood to explain a gym, she said, "You are . . . magnificent."

The word sounded hollow. Silly, really. But he was, and Hannah couldn't think of any other word to describe him.

"Stay," he said in response.

She froze. "What did you say?"

He leaned down and kissed her, his lips silencing her protest in the most enticing way possible. When he pulled away, she simply stared at him.

"Don't answer me now. I know what you will say."

Indeed, the only answer could be no if there was a way for her to go back and find her sisters.

"But just think on it. When my men return . . . answer me then."

He slipped his hand underneath her chemise again, and this time it did not stop. It trailed over her hips and toward her breast, where it finally paused.

Tristan's groan emboldened her. She moved her hand toward the evidence of his need.

"Let me pleasure you, Tristan."

He'd given without taking, but now it was his turn.

His hand stilled on her breast.

The need to pleasure him roared through her body. "What is it?"

Her words had affected him in some way—on some level beyond mere pleasure. Maybe he would explain it to her, maybe not. But she intended to show him how he affected her.

Hannah pulled his hand down so it rested at his side. Then, taking him by surprise, which was the only way she'd be able to overpower him, Hannah pushed him flat on the bed and straddled him.

"I'd like nothing more than to feel you inside me, Tristan."

How was that for honesty?

"But we both know that can't happen," she added.

She began to move against him, the hardness she felt even more pronounced against the sensitive spot that he had just brought to an exquisite climax.

"I'd have nabbed a condom had I known . . ." She shook her head at his confusion. "Never mind."

Hannah reached down and untied the laces that would free him from confinement. These were nothing like the skintight pantyhose women wore in the twenty-first. Much looser, though still tight enough to accentuate every muscle, they were also tied at the top. Elastic was apparently still a thing of the future.

He watched her the entire time, and Hannah wished she could take back her words. She'd never been this turned on in her life. Even lying prone on the bed, in arguably the most compromising position there was, Tristan exuded strength and confidence.

But at this moment, he was at her mercy.

She stopped just before her hand slipped inside his hose. Jumping up, she ran to the washstand and brought back a cloth and laid it strategically on top of him.

"Hannah Sutton . . . where did you come from?"

She smiled, a wicked side she didn't know she possessed suddenly wanting to tease him a bit. "You know the answer to that."

Even so, he looked at her as if this was the first time a woman had done this to him. Which, of course, could not be true given where he'd been raised and how he'd acquired his considerable skills.

She allowed only the tips of her fingers to slip inside, barely touching the flesh beneath. He knew what she was about, but he didn't move. He didn't attempt to guide her hand as most men would have done by now. His restrained response sent a jolt of desire down to her very core.

"Are women not so . . . forward . . . in your time?"

His eyes narrowed. "No. Most are not."

She inched her fingertips just a bit lower. This time, she reached inside and pulled down the cloth that separated them. Hannah couldn't help but look down. And while there was only a dim flicker of light in the darkened room, it was enough.

She swallowed and met his eyes once again. Hannah had thought she was the one in control, but she wasn't so sure anymore. Right now, if he asked her again to stay, she might be tempted to say yes. There was more than lust in his eyes as he calmly waited for her to continue.

She knew that look. In the past, it had always scared her, but now . . .

Wrapping her hand around him, she was finally rewarded with the slightest crack in his armor. When she began to move her hand, Tristan lifted his chin just slightly. She took her cues from his expression, watching as carefully as possible for the slightest changes so she could do more of what he seemed to like. When he finally closed his eyes, his hips moving into her, Hannah dealt him the ultimate blow.

"Tristan?"

He opened his eyes and looked at her.

She didn't stop.

But Hannah did open her mouth, just slightly, suggestively. She touched the tip of her tongue to her upper lip and enjoyed watching Tristan come apart.

And she'd thought him magnificent before.

They say true seduction comes from giving, not receiving, but Hannah had never been convinced of that before this moment.

The man splayed beneath her had walked casually back to their camp with blood dripping from his sword . . . He'd earned respect, despite his humble beginnings, from dozens of men who'd pledged to follow him into battle . . .

Watching him, pleasuring him, making him gasp . . . Hannah had never felt as powerful in her life. Which went against everything she believed. She didn't need a man to feel complete. And certainly her greatest accomplishment had been getting into Yale. Or running a successful business. Not . . . this. Why should she feel so—

No. No, no, no, no, no!

Hannah was not in love with him. Most certainly not.

"Hannah?"

He brought her attention back to him.

"Aye, Tristan?"

He looked at her with such intensity her belly jittered with anticipation.

"You're not going back."

15

$\mathcal{T}$ristan attempted to concentrate, but the thought of the previous night with Hannah made it difficult. He sat opposite Walter and John, rubbing his head as he listened to their argument. He hadn't the heart for the familiar talk of Sutherland and the truce. He'd left Hannah's room soon after making his rash declaration. She hadn't answered him, but it was just as well. The answer would be one he'd not like. Tristan knew she would never agree to stay without knowing the fate of her sisters. But even without them, he reminded himself, she had another life, in another time.

And yet the thought of Saxford Castle without her . . .

"My lord," John said, interrupting his thoughts. "If we do not at least attempt to speak to Sutherland—"

"The time for talk is long over, John," Tristan said. "Sutherland has made it clear he will not honor the conditions of the treaty once it expires. His own warden is powerless to stop him. No one wants war—"

"Sutherland does."

Tristan shot Walter a look. He was on his side, and the

blasted man didn't even realize it. The merest whisper of words like "talk" or "peace" would throw Walter into a fit of anger.

They sat in Tristan's solar, a room designed for this very type of meeting. Adjacent to his bedchamber, it had a high window that flooded the room with light. Just now, Tristan wished he could climb out of it and away from this discussion.

And it had nothing to do with him wanting to see Hannah.

"Once blood is shed, the only way forward will be more blood," John said. "Our allies are well-meaning—"

"But only Saxford stands directly in Sutherland's path," Tristan finished for him. It was a refrain he'd heard many times. "I am here for one purpose," he said, ending the discussion. "To keep Clan Sutherland at bay. Kenton has given us leave to deal with him as we choose. We can call on his men when they are needed. But on this, I agree with Walter."

John muttered a curse under his breath. "So we sit and wait. For the inevitable."

Tristan understood the man's frustration, but any attempt to make peace with Sutherland would merely make them look weak. The lord had made his position known. "We prepare, as we've done."

"Extra men in the village, patrols . . ." John sighed.

Again, Tristan agreed it was not ideal. But it was Sutherland who'd insisted on this course, not them.

He stood. "Aye, and so we wait."

Walter and John stood with him and took his cue. After they left, Tristan walked toward the window, its wooden shutters opened wide. He watched the sea below for a few moments, remembering the first time he'd taken in this very view. He'd had so much to prove back then. And whether the people of Saxford had mocked him in the beginning, or if he'd only imagined it so, Tristan would never be sure. He only knew that he'd wasted too much time questioning himself—a mistake he would not make again.

Striding from the room, Tristan went off in search of Hannah. Of course, it would not take long to find the woman who would stand out in any crowd. He left the main keep and squinted against the bright midday sun as he stepped through the arched stone entranceway and began to descend the stairs. Voices at the bottom reached him, slowing his steps.

"Nay, my lady. I will not have you—"

"Listen to me, Cook. I understand you are not accustomed to this . . ."

He knew he should either continue down the stone stairway or turn around, but Tristan did neither. He listened to Hannah's conversation with the ornery cook, in awe at how authoritatively she spoke to him. None before her, other than Tristan himself and perhaps Gerard, had ever dared to do so.

"I've been usin' bread to thicken sauces for longer than you've been alive."

Although his words were harsh, his tone anything but kind, Hannah laughed.

"And how did the squeeze of lemon turn out? That is to say, the sauce last eve—"

"But flour? Beggin' your pardon, my lady . . ."

Begging your pardon? Had that truly come from Cook's mouth? Tristan took one more step down, hardly able to believe what he was hearing. So the rumors were, in fact, true?

"Aye, flour."

She sounded less like an American, as she called herself, each day.

"If it was good enough for the Romans, it's good enough for you. Do you have any idea how much time this will save you?"

"Ach, girl. I'll try it this once." Cook did not sound pleased by the prospect.

"And you will not be disappointed. Here, give it to me—"

"You'll be telling me what to do *and* doin' it yourself? Nay . . ."

He could not hear the rest of Cook's grumbling, but it seemed a good time to make his presence known. Tristan walked down the remainder of the stairs and was about to turn the corner to enter the kitchen when Hannah saw him. He gestured for her to join him. After disappearing for a moment, she reappeared and made her way up the stairs.

They walked out of the entranceway and into the bailey. Tristan's heartbeat quickened, as it did every time they stood this close.

"Do you have time for a walk?"

He had gone to sleep last eve thinking of being inside her. Had woken up thinking of it too. And now, standing so close he could smell the scent that was uniquely Hannah . . .

A walk on the beach had seemed like a good idea when he was alone looking out the window. Now Tristan wasn't so sure

"I never did ask how you've begun to bring the grumpiest man in all of Saxford to your side . . ."

Her sideways glance made him chuckle.

"I'm speaking of Cook, not me. In fact, some say I am downright jovial."

Tristan's chest swelled at the sound of Hannah's laughter. "That's not the word I'd use to describe you."

As they made their way down the path that led away from the castle, Tristan found himself looking toward the spot where he'd first seen Hannah. Resisting the urge to ask which words she *would* use, he nodded toward the stretch of sand.

"What is the first thing you remember?"

Hannah frowned. "Feeling dizzy. At first I thought I was back home. When I saw your men . . ." She shook her head. "I didn't know what to think."

Tristan turned as they reached the spot, trying to look back at the castle from a newcomer's eyes.

"You must have been scared."

"Scared, confused . . . I really did think your men were reenactors." She'd explained the concept to him days ago, and he'd had a laugh over everything they'd gotten wrong. The clothing was much less practical, table manners much more enlightened. If the twenty-first-century vision of the middle ages was accurate in some ways, in others, it was downright the opposite of the truth. "If I ever do get back . . ."

She stopped and looked up at him through her thick lashes. "I should not have said that."

"Your decisions are your own. But I do want you to know—"

"Tristan, please."

"Just listen."

He took her hands in his, the sound of soft lapping of water behind him. The soothing sound and her big green eyes lulled him into a gentleness he hadn't known he possessed.

"I want you to understand," he started. "When I told you to stay—"

Hannah shook her head. The stubborn woman simply would not listen.

So he kissed her. He pressed his lips against hers, his tongue demanding entry. She opened for him, her sweet taste fanning the fire inside him into an inferno.

He couldn't get enough of her. His hands found the

mounds that pressed against them, his desire to feel them against his skin restrained only by the unfortunate cut of her gown. He groaned when her hands lowered from his back to his buttocks, a saucy squeeze followed by her pressing him closer. She was forward, but no more so than he. She met his passion with her own at each turn, and Tristan didn't know how long he could last without claiming the ultimate prize.

He released her as a defense against his own impulses. Before they went any further, he needed her to understand . . .

"My men should be back any day, and before they return, you should know what I'm asking of you, Hannah. When I asked you to stay, I meant as my wife."

Her eyes widened.

"Before I met you, I didn't think much of the institution of marriage. I had seen too many husbands break their vows at The Swan. But you have opened my eyes, Hannah, and when I look to the future, it seems empty without you in it."

He stopped short of saying the one thing he'd never thought to say to a woman. But if love meant caring for someone more than you did yourself, then he was in love with Hannah Sutton. Because he wanted Hannah to stay more than anything, but if faced with the choice of her staying or finding her beloved sisters, he would gladly give her up.

Tristan saw Gerard riding toward them before he heard him. The sound of the sea drowned out his steward's shouted words, but something was clearly wrong. Hannah must have seen it in his eyes, because she turned back toward the path leading to the castle.

"My lord!"

Tristan watched as the hooves of Gerard's horse kicked up sand all around him.

"You're needed immediately at the castle."

"What is it?"

"Reivers," Gerard said. "Three of them. They say Sutherland has already told his men the truce is over, that any Scot found guilty of reiving Saxford land will be rewarded rather than brought to the warden for justice. Take my horse. You're needed back at the castle."

"That bastard." He glanced at Hannah. "We must—"

"Go," she said. "Go ahead. I will follow you."

Gerard was already dismounting.

Tristan took the reins, and with a final quick glance at his best friend and the woman he loved, he made his way toward the keep.

<hr />

HANNAH SAT at the front of the hall for the midday meal, looking toward the entrance each time she heard new voices. Neither Tristan nor Gerard had yet made an appearance, and she feared the worst.

The largest meal of the day, dinner typically consisted of multiple courses and boasted a hall filled to capacity with retainers, servants and sometimes, it seemed, just about every person who lived and worked at Saxford.

But not today.

Fewer people, less chatter, and the worst . . . the dour looks those that did remain seemed to be giving each other.

A very different feel had descended on the castle since Gerard had brought news of the reivers, and Hannah couldn't help but wonder if she was half-crazed to even consider staying here. Danger was coming, that much was clear. And she felt she was betraying her sisters and her parents' memory by even considering Tristan's plea. And yet she had thought of nothing else . . .

"More ale, my lady?"

Hannah tried to smile at the servant as she spotted Durwin, who'd just entered the hall and was making his way toward her.

"No, thank you."

They drank ale like water around here, and though it tasted very different and was clearly not as potent as beer, she still could not get used to the idea of drinking it all day long.

"Pardon, my lady."

The squire had reached the dais and, after a quick bow, said, "My lord sent me to inform you he'll not be at the meal."

Despite the fact that she'd been looking up every two minutes, Hannah had already guessed as much.

"Thank you for informing me, Durwin."

The squire's eyes darted away from her to the side of the hall, where two female maids stood giggling. Hannah assumed he might be looking at them in a coming-of-age-type way until he frowned.

"Is all well?" she asked.

"'Tis not my place, my lady. But Gerard is with my lord and . . ." He shrugged.

"What is it?" Something was clearly troubling him.

One of the girls motioned to the cupbearer, who seemed to be practically running through the hall in an effort to fill each person's mug.

"They should be helping," he said. Then, shaking his head, Durwin apologized. "As I said, 'tis not my place. Pardon, my lady."

With that, the squire left, but Hannah continued to watch the two maids. Not only were they not doing their jobs, but the two young ladies appeared to be teasing the cupbearer as he did the work of all three of them. Apparently mean girls were not a twenty-first-century phenomenon.

If it wasn't Durwin's place to intervene, it certainly wasn't hers. But tolerating inefficiency had never been one of her strong suits. By the end of the meal, Hannah had had enough. She stood and made her way toward them.

Neither girl paid her any attention until she was practically standing on top of them.

"Good day," she said through a forced smile.

Both girls presented a slight bow and mumbled a greeting. Hannah followed their gaze to the cupbearer.

"How lucky he is," she said, watching him work, "to be singled out by the lord in such a way."

Certainly the social structure she'd found here at Saxford was very different, but people were people. No matter when and where they came from. And one thing had not changed in hundreds of years. Some people would not work hard without added motivation.

"Singled out? I don't understand," the blonde one said, exchanging a wide-eyed look with her friend.

"My lord has noticed how hard he works and is planning something special to thank him for his efforts."

What that something special might be . . . well, Tristan could figure it out.

"Good day," she said, quitting while she was ahead.

One conversation would certainly not change their behavior for good. But it was a start.

She made her way from the hall toward the kitchen to compliment Cook on another fine meal. The man was certainly ornery, but she liked him despite it. Or maybe because of it.

Hannah stopped as two men on horseback rode toward the stable. Their demeanor was quite serious. Likely it had something to do with Sutherland's decree. The man really did sound like the bastard Tristan had accused him of being. On the other hand, if the feud really had been going on for generations, he probably felt like there was no other path forward. Even in her time people confused aggression for leadership. In reality, there were so many different ways to be strong. Sometimes, her father had said, being strong meant compromising with others.

Hannah wasn't the only one in her family to have won an award recognizing excellence in business—she had learned from the best. A flower shop in Maine, an event planning partnership in Boston, and a castle in Saxford. All had one thing in common. People.

People, she realized suddenly, who were at risk. Including herself. Hannah should be more scared, but instead she worried for her sisters.

She had to find them.

Nothing else matters. Not even him.

If she kept repeating the phrase to herself, perhaps it would become true.

16

How could he have ever asked Hannah to stay on the eve of certain war?

More messengers had arrived after the first group, and the situation was worse than he had first thought.

The treaty was over.

It seemed the chief wasn't concerned with particulars such as the date of the truce's expiration. This time, the messengers were not reivers spreading possible rumors, but two of Tristan's own clansmen. That Sutherland had announced his decision so openly, so publicly, was a fatal blow to the ten years' peace.

The border between Saxford and Sutherland was about to descend into chaos again. And there was nothing he could do to stop it.

Having missed both meals, Tristan climbed down the stone stairs to see what Cook could muster up for him. Even though the sun had set hours ago, he knew the man would still be hard at work. The smell of freshly baked bread wafting from the kitchen confirmed it.

The soft light of the oven's fire greeted him. As expected, Cook stood alone in the center of the large space, kneading dough.

Of course Hannah would not be here at this time of night. "You've no one to help you finish?"

The gray-haired servant did not look up.

"Finish? Why?" he asked gruffly, continuing his task.

"So you can rest."

As soon as he said it, Tristan could have kicked himself. Cook had told him more than once why he spent every waking moment in the kitchen. But still, he always hoped something . . . someone . . . would change the old man's mind.

"Rest," Cook scoffed.

Tristan reached for a finished loaf of rye bread and, to Cook's obvious dismay, tore off half of it.

"Take it all," the older man said. "What am I to do with the rest of it?"

Tristan returned the remainder of the loaf to the table. "Serve it. Eat it. It is, after all, what you typically do—"

"Not like that."

Finally, Cook looked up. His brown eyes were tired, and perhaps resigned. So many of Saxford's people had lived their entire lives here. They and their families had watched it change hands over the last hundred years. Scottish . . . English . . . and then an absentee English lord until Kenton finally obtained it from the king. Tristan vowed the people of Saxford would never worry for their safety again.

"I will not let them take Saxford," he said.

And meant it.

Cook sighed, pulled his hands away from his work and looked up once again. And then the most miraculous thing happened. The corner of his mouth actually lifted, if only slightly.

A smile?

"I know," Cook said.

The half-smile was gone. But it had been there, and Tristan considered it a victory. Perhaps he should leave it at that. After all, Tristan had not been here when Cook's wife and newborn daughter died during childbirth. But the man's losses still affected him these many years later, and Tristan had never spoken of it to him. Perhaps it was time.

"You're a good man," he said honestly. "And a talented one. They would have been proud."

Cook didn't respond, but neither did he throw a pot or growl. It felt like another victory, and Tristan turned to leave.

"She said the same. Just this mornin'."

Tristan stopped just as he hunched under the arched opening to the stairwell that led back outside.

"She?" he asked without turning around.

"My lady," Cook said, the affection in his voice unmistakable.

Tristan's chest swelled with pride as he turned around. This time, there was no mistaking it. Cook grinned like a squire the day before his dubbing ceremony.

"*They* sent her," he said. Tristan's feet were weighed to the ground. He couldn't move. He could hardly breathe. Something about Cook's words . . . the idea was as absurd as, well, her being here at all. Yet somehow Tristan knew it was true. Whether it was their spirit, some strange magic at the waterfall, or both, Hannah was meant to be here. With him.

He couldn't answer, so instead Tristan attempted a smile before taking his leave. And though he'd once convinced himself that leaving Saxford might be best for Hannah after all, he no longer believed as much.

He needed to see her.

Immediately.

HANNAH HAD NOT MEANT to leave the hall prematurely, but she didn't feel like returning after her talk with the two maids. Privacy was difficult to come by in a castle, with the exception of the bedchambers, which were afforded to very few. Not ready to return to her room, she found herself wandering the corridors.

Toward Tristan.

Hannah stopped, waiting for some kind of divine intervention to guide her. She wasn't one to trust herself to the hand of fate or astronomy or any other superstitious nonsense . . . but then again, she had traveled back in time.

Despite herself, she had begun to imagine what saying yes to Tristan's unconventional proposal would be like. The idea was not an unpleasant one. In fact, there was much to recommend it. Including Tristan himself. On the other hand, even if—and that was a big if—she decided to stay, would she still wish to do so if her sisters were found and wanted to return if such a thing were possible? And these were obviously dangerous times, and she remembered quite clearly that life expectancy had been much shorter in the Middle Ages. Could she stay here, without antibiotics or safe birthing practices, and give up all that she'd built back home?

"Finally . . ." Tristan's squire panted as he ran up to her. Beads of sweat dotted his brow.

"What is it?" Something was very wrong.

"I looked in your chamber and in the kitchens. My lord was beginning to worry . . . the men are back . . . he couldn't find you." The boy's words jumbled into each other.

"What did you say?" She held her breath as she waited for him to speak.

"I looked everywhere—"

"Nay, about the men?"

Durwin blinked as he finally caught his breath. They both looked up to a wall torch that flickered as if a gust of wind had caught it. What the hell was that? They were indoors and far from any window or door.

"Aye, the men. My lord requests your presence immediately."

Calm down, Hannah. They probably did not discover anything.

"Take me to him," she said, picking up her overly elaborate skirts.

They practically ran to Tristan's solar, a room she'd only been to once before. Just as they arrived, Hannah felt his presence behind them.

"Thank you, Durwin," he said, his greeting also a dismissal. The boy bowed and left as she turned around.

Hannah prided herself on being independent. She didn't need a man, could manage very well all by her lonesome. But her body had apparently not received the message, because when Tristan looked at her that way—like she was the only woman in this or any time—she wanted to wrap her arms around him and stay by his side for eternity.

"Are you ready?"

She swallowed. No, not really. "I suppose."

He took a step toward her, giving her a better view of his face, and she saw faint lines around his eyes where there were usually none. Was he tired? Worried? What was it like to know you would be leading your men to battle at any time? It wasn't a responsibility she envied.

"Are they in there?" she asked, already knowing the answer.

Tristan nodded. When he reached for her, Hannah's shoulders relaxed, the tension instantly melting away.

Her pulse raced as he leaned down to kiss her, the tender caress most welcome.

After the too-quick kiss, Tristan pulled back. He wanted

to say something, and she did as well, yet neither of them did. They stood just inches apart, silent, until he finally took a step back. The air around them seemed to crackle with energy.

"Come," he said, stepping in front of her. Hannah held her breath as he pushed the door open.

17

*H*annah peered around Tristan, frantically scanning the room. Empty, but for the two men who'd been sent to seek information. Only then did Hannah realize she'd expected—hoped—her sisters would be standing in the solar.

Suddenly, it registered that Tristan and the scouts were all watching her. He must have introduced her to them.

"Good eve, sirs," she said, not having caught their names.

They bowed, murmuring their welcome. Were the men brothers? They looked almost like twins with their bushy brown hair and full beards. And they were nearly as tall as Tristan, though one was just slightly smaller than the other.

"What did you find?" Tristan said, thankfully not wasting any time.

When both men looked at her, Hannah's heart began to race once again. They knew something. She could feel it.

"We spoke to many about the falls, inquired after the two women you had described."

"And?" Rude, undoubtedly, but she couldn't help it. Hannah was just about ready to burst.

"There are rumors." The smaller brother frowned.

"What rumors?" she asked.

"All who knew of Leannan Falls had a different tale to tell," the bigger brother said.

The two exchanged an odd look, and the smaller man spoke next. "Some say a faerie lives beneath the water, and others insist she had a lover, a knight—"

"But all agree there is something . . . special . . . about those falls," finished the bigger one.

"Special?" she and Tristan said in unison. Perhaps this meant her sisters had indeed come through the falls with her.

Big brother shifted, as if speaking of such things meant he himself believed them. "Magical," he said, mumbling the word.

Little brother rolled his eyes. "As I said, some insist a faerie lives beneath the water and that she once fell in love with a man, a knight, and had the chance to become human to be with him."

"And though she loved him"—big brother warmed to the topic—"she decided to remain a faerie, vowing to bring true love together for all of eternity."

Hannah froze.

"Nonsense, of course," he added. "How exactly does a faerie who lives beneath the water accomplish such a thing?"

But Hannah already knew the answer.

Little brother shrugged his shoulders. "A merchant in Auld Town claimed the knight visited her on the banks of the falls every day until he died."

Hannah would have been as skeptical as the brothers if not for the fact that she'd literally fallen through the water into the fourteenth century. This talk of healing properties and an ancient legend reminded her of the innkeeper's words on the morning she and her sisters left for Leannan Falls—the falls will bring soulmates together. A different story, but a legend nonetheless. Rumors about the falls had persisted for at least six hundred years.

Hannah waited expectantly.

"Then, on our last day in Edinburgh, our inquiries led us to an old woman—"

"An odd old woman," little brother added.

"Who claimed to have knowledge of Lady Hannah and her sisters." He turned to Tristan. "It took all of the coin you gave us to retrieve that information."

"What did the woman say?" he asked.

It seemed she was not the only impatient one.

"She was reluctant to speak to us. All we could gather from her was that 'three women arrived in Scotland' and that 'they were meant to be here.'"

"Some called her a seer, others a witch. But most agreed her information was usually sound."

"Hannah?" Tristan said, his tone unreadable.

She looked back up. "Thank you," she said to the men. "Thank you for your help."

Their strange experience would not allay their curiosity about her, but Hannah did not care. If this woman was right, they were here. Her sisters were really here.

"You've done well," Tristan said, "but you're to tell no one what you've said in this chamber."

"My lord," both men said with a slight bow. They turned to leave and shut the door behind them.

Hannah's mouth felt like she'd just drunk ten cupfuls of tea. She moistened her lips and blinked, trying to focus on Tristan.

"Hannah?"

The sound of his concerned voice broke the spell, and she threw her arms around him. She wanted to jump up and down and scream with delight.

"They're here!" she said finally. "They're here," she said,

repeating it again and again until she was nearly dizzy with excitement, arms still wrapped around Tristan.

And then she remembered the legend. Could it be true? Could Tristan possibly be destined for her?

Hannah pulled away and looked up at Tristan. His expression told her he knew. Somehow, he knew the legend was true, just as she did.

Now what were they to do about it?

*H*annah had to seek news of her sisters.

Unfortunately, she hardly had a chance to discuss the matter with Tristan. Mere moments after they'd learned her sisters had come through the falls, Tristan had been informed of an attack.

Sutherland had made good on his threats, and worse, new rumors warned of an imminent attack on the village. Tristan had left, telling her he would return the next night. When the following evening came and went, Hannah began to worry. Had something happened to him? Why would he stay in the village, without protection, rather than behind the walls of the castle where it was safe?

The preparations had taken on a furious pace, leaving Hannah to twiddle her thumbs in the meantime. She'd learned from Gerard that no one was to leave the castle walls. It felt as if danger lurked on every side.

She had just decided to see if Cook needed help when she heard a familiar voice addressing her. "There you are."

Turning, Hannah's heart lurched at the sight of him. This was neither a bawd's son nor an armorer's apprentice. He may have been both, once, but the man who stood in front of her now was an English lord from head to foot . . . a medieval knight if she'd ever seen one. He wore a surcoat of green and gold, Saxford colors, his sword hanging so casually by his side that Hannah could almost forget it was a weapon in truth and not a showpiece.

The sun shone behind him, and Hannah had to hold up her hand to shield her eyes. She had not seen him since the day they'd learned about the legend of the falls.

"I came to tell you that I'm leaving," he said. This man, the lord, had no extra words or loving whispers for her today. He was all business.

"Oh," she said. Despite how much she'd longed to speak with him, to discuss the scouts' findings with him, words suddenly failed her.

"The latest rumors proved false . . . all is well. For now. But I cannot stay here and wait for the next threat to come from Sutherland. He's agreed to a meeting, and I ride out immediately."

He reached out then and grabbed her by the arm, the movement so sudden Hannah hardly had time to react before he moved them to an opening between the main keep and the eastern wall of the kitchen.

"We have not had a chance to talk—"

"You have more important matters to address," she said, knowing it was true but wanting to speak about what had happened anyway.

"You are important," he said, and Hannah's heart soared. "As soon as this is over, we will travel to Edinburgh ourselves," he said. "We will find your sisters."

"Tristan," she began, "I don't know what's happening. You left so quickly, and Gerard . . ." She shrugged. "He doesn't tell me much."

"What do you want to know?" To his credit, Tristan looked genuinely confused.

"I want to know what is happening. Why you were gone for two nights? What is Sutherland planning and how are you going to counter him? I want to know if we're safe. If I were to consider staying . . ."

His eyes widened.

"I need to know. Everything."

Tristan took her hands, engulfing them with his own. "If your sisters are truly here . . ."

He didn't finish, and Hannah understood what he meant. He thought she would find a way to leave with them. She couldn't say it aloud herself, but she'd thought of little else. She'd even made up a mental pros and cons list—reasons to stay or go.

"I don't know," she said. "Everything is so different now."

When he squeezed her hands, all of her "reasons to go" list fell by the wayside. Medicine, refrigeration, beer that actually tasted like beer . . . none of it mattered.

Except for one problem, something that had stood out to her these last lonely days.

"Things are different in your time, relationships are different. If we were together in the twenty-first century, I would know as much as you do about this truce and the implications of it falling apart. We'd have discussed it, and possible solutions, including the most obvious one."

The poor guy looked as confused as ever.

"*Peace*," she said. "You haven't once mentioned the possibility of forming a peace accord with Sutherland. Of ending this feud—"

"Ending it?" Tristan's laugh was forced. Bitter.

He dropped her hands.

"He has no interest in ending the feud. I go to set terms for battle. Sutherland has already proven—"

"That he is capable of some restraint. He honored the treaty until now."

Tristan's eyes had narrowed, and he looked at her with a combination of shock and disdain. Though he seemed to respect her, he wasn't showing much respect for her opinion in this. His hatred of the man had blinded him.

"He is a bastard, one intent on revenge for what happened ten years ago."

"But have you or Lord Kenton even tried? Remember when I told you about that feud in my time—"

"Hannah, this is not your time," he said, more harshly than she would have liked.

"I know very well it isn't," she said.

"As for the rest of it, I have a marshal to worry about our safety. And a steward to care for the castle. You need only—"

"Sit in my bedchamber learning to embroider?" She very nearly spat out the words.

"My lord," Walter called, peering beyond the wall at them. "All is ready."

"I will be but a moment," Tristan said.

Though he looked curious—perhaps he'd heard her last words—Walter merely nodded to her and walked away. As soon as he was gone, Tristan turned back to her. "Hannah, I must go."

He reached for her, but Hannah pulled away. It would do no good to pretend all was well. "Then go," she said, knowing she was being cross.

He clearly didn't want to leave. And truth be told, she didn't want him to go like this either. But maybe it was for the best. In his own way, he seemed to agree with Kenton about how a woman should be treated—and where a woman's place was. The home.

"If you're worried for your safety," he said, "do not be. Saxford has been heavily fortified in recent years."

She was less concerned for her safety than she was for her pride, but Hannah remained quiet.

"Go," she repeated.

And please come back safely so that I might give you a proper goodbye.

With a bow, Tristan left.

———

TRISTAN HANDED the two hares he'd snared to one of his men, ignoring Walter's disapproving glance. The marshal didn't take the hint.

"How can I protect you, my lord, if you insist on leaving camp?"

"I can protect myself," he insisted.

Walter's indisposition came down to his fervent dislike of anything resembling diplomacy with Sutherland. Two of the Scotsman's own men had ridden to the village to invite him to a meeting with their master. The chief knew, as he did, a new era would begin, one of constant battles and reiving on both sides of the border. He'd proposed the meeting so they could set the terms of their feud. Walter worried it was a trap, but Tristan did not. Sutherland, though a bastard, was an honorable one.

Their disagreement had put Walter in a foul mood, and his argument with Hannah had done the same for him. In all, it had been a miserable journey with the next day promising more of the same.

"We should have brought more than twenty men," Walter grumbled, unhappy with the size of their retinue as well. Tristan looked around at their makeshift camp as the marshal continued to scowl at him.

"I thought you said we never should have come."

The observation deepened his marshal's scowl. Tristan

glanced toward the fire, where John stood among the men. If it were not for his captain, Tristan might have been inclined to agree. And then, of course, there was Hannah.

He had not forgotten their talk. It had physically pained him to part from her that way, especially after the revelation about her sisters.

"Something else is wrong," Walter said.

Of course, he was right.

"Tomorrow," he tried to pacify him, "Saxford's future will be—"

"Nay, something else."

Tristan remained silent, watching the men as they jested with one another while they ate.

"The woman."

Tristan folded his arms. "She has a name."

"Hannah. A most unusual name for a woman."

"Aye, but not for a man?" he jested.

Walter did not laugh. "You know more than you are telling us," he said. It was a fact, not an accusation.

Tristan sighed. "I would tell you if I could. But on this, you will just have to trust me."

The older man grunted and bent down to pick up a stick. He pulled out his knife and began to cut thin pieces of it away. He'd seen his marshal do that same thing hundreds of times before. Walter had difficulty remaining still for long.

"Will you marry her?"

No other question would have surprised him more.

"Maybe," he answered honestly. Though it was likely she would not have him, his wishes had not changed. "She's accustomed to . . . other places. Not staying in one place for long." It was as close to the truth as he could get.

"She is unlike other women," the marshal said. "But I like her. She . . . knows things."

Walter had managed to surprise him. He liked few people,

and trusted even fewer. It seemed Cook was not the only person at Saxford to see what he had, to understand Hannah was unlike any other.

"As do I."

In fact, he loved her. Tristan loved everything about Hannah Sutton. She was beautiful, of course, but also passionate and kind. And intelligent. He smiled. She'd make an excellent steward. If she were lady of Saxford, she and Gerard would get along well. She *did* know things, as Walter said, though he could not tell him how.

Tristan froze.

He'd dismissed her. Though she had proven herself capable in so many ways—from dealing with Cook to acclimating herself to an entirely different century—Tristan had not listened to her advice about Sutherland.

She was not a woman of his time, which was one of the things he loved most about her, and yet he'd treated her as he would a simpering lady. But could he really do as she asked? He had spent the last ten years proving his strength to everyone around him. Could he really put himself, and his people, in such a position of weakness?

How much do you really value her advice?

He looked at Walter, who seemed to sense Tristan was about to say something he would not like. And he was right. Tristan knew what he had to do.

19

*H*annah was going to Edinburgh.

She would track down the woman who somehow knew about them, and she would find her sisters. As for Tristan . . . Hannah tried not to think about him. Or the hole that was left where her heart used to be. Or the feel of his arms around her . . . or the way their bodies melded perfectly together.

No! Stop it, Hannah!

She'd thought about it from every angle these past two days, and as much as she loved him, Hannah simply could not stay here. Too many differences stood between them—roughly six hundred years' worth.

Hannah entered the hall, pleased to see how much brighter it looked after all of the tapestries had been taken down, beaten, and replaced. Coupled with a good wall washing with lye soap, it was a much-needed improvement. Though she made the suggestion, Hannah was not sure it would be well-received.

"Good den, my lady." The greeting came from one of the two formerly negligent maids. Though the two were not completely reformed, Hannah was pleased to see they were at least doing the job they'd been given—sprinkling the new rushes with chamomile and mint.

As she made her way to the head table, every head turned toward the entrance. When she sat on the dais, she caught sight of what—or rather who—commanded their attention. Cook rarely left the kitchen. Even during celebrations, when Gerard had apparently begged the man to give over his duties and be celebrated in the hall for his culinary excellence, he elected to remain "where he belonged."

Yet here he was, carrying the roasted duck he'd bragged about that morn on a large wooden tray. Hannah smiled, and when Cook placed the tray on the table in front of her, she was sure to let him know how much she appreciated his effort.

"You have made my day," she said. The silence had broken at last, and the people of Saxford had begun to whisper to each other as they stared at Cook.

"They are surprised is all," she said, wanting to encourage his foray out from the kitchen. "And you have made me the merriest woman in the world."

He repeated the quote she'd shared with him the day before. "'If more of us valued food and cheer and song—'"

"'Above hoarded gold, it would be a merrier world,'" she finished, smiling. Tolkien wouldn't write those words for many, many years, but she had thought the sentiment a fitting encouragement for Cook, who, for all of his bluster, did not seem to recognize his value to Saxford.

A quick glance at Gerard, who stood off to the side, confirmed that he was pleased by Cook's efforts.

"A wise and beautiful woman," Cook said with a bow. "My lady."

He left as quickly as he'd come. His gesture had put a smile on her face, but that smile slowly faded as she realized she would be leaving him too—and just when he was starting to come out of what had surely been a deep depression. After a respectable amount of time passed, she stood and left the hall, stricken with the fact that she would be abandoning someone who needed her.

She contemplated the problem as she roamed through the keep. Perhaps Gerard could take over where she'd left off?

Hannah stopped walking, surprised to see the great big door in front of her. How had she come to be here? When she'd left the hall, Hannah had not paid much attention to where she was going, but an empty bedchamber belonging to the Lord of Saxford was certainly not her destination. Curious, she pushed open the door and entered the room. No fire had been lit since Tristan was not expected back yet. The only illumination was a single torch, and it was so dark she could barely see anything beyond the outlines of furniture. Still, she could not bring herself to leave. Hannah thought of the time she'd attempted to explain the concept of dating to Tristan. And of how he'd arranged the date at the tavern as a surprise for her.

A date with a medieval knight.

She laughed aloud at the absurdity of it.

"First I find you lying on the shore as if you'd washed up from the North Sea—"

It couldn't be . . .

"—and now I find you in my bedchamber, laughing into the darkness."

Tristan.

HE HAD THOUGHT she had left.

Tristan had pushed his men so they would return by nightfall. When the sun set, unrelenting, he pushed them further. Desperate to get back to Saxford . . . to Hannah. By the time they rode through the gates, his marshal was not the only one questioning his soundness of mind.

When he entered the great hall and saw the empty head table, Tristan did not stop to ask questions. He made his way to her chamber, doubt beginning to nag at him. When he opened the door and saw the room empty, Tristan feared he was too late. Good sense prevailed then, and he questioned the first servants he could find and was informed Hannah had been at the meal just moments earlier.

If there had been any doubt before, Tristan knew in those brief but excruciating moments that he did, indeed, love her.

He wanted to marry her.

The sight of her in his room had filled him with an intoxicating blend of relief and joy. Tristan did not waste a moment before going to her. He did not even give her time to turn around. He placed the lantern he'd taken from the hall on the table beside him and went to her. Grabbing a handful of her hair and moving it to the side, Tristan breathed in the faint scent of mint that now suffused his hall. He'd noticed the changes there—change Hannah had undoubtedly prompted—and took it as yet another sign that she was destined to run Saxford with him.

"Tristan," she whispered, her voice soothing his very soul. "What are you doing?"

He brought his hands around to her front and cupped both of her breasts with his hands.

"Isn't it obvious?" This time, he did squeeze, though gently. He let his thumbs dip inside the top of her gown.

"When you left—"

"I was a fool," he said, rubbing the tips of his thumbs back and forth, the soft flesh teasing him. And so he teased back. He brought his lips closer to her ear. "I should have listened to you. I've always loved women—"

"Now hardly seems the time to remind me."

"Admired them for their beauty," he continued. "And known they were much cleverer than me."

He paused, but only to kiss the tender spot just under her ear. "And you, the cleverest of all."

Another kiss, but a bit harder this time. He began to move his hands as well, needing to reassure himself that she was here, that he might yet convince her to stay with him.

"You told me to speak to Sutherland, but I dismissed the idea, not wanting to appear weak."

"Weakness has nothing to do with—"

"Allow me to finish."

He pressed her closer to him.

"I was wrong," he said against her neck. "But you were as well. This is not your time, but it can be. Saxford needs you. I need you. I believe in things I never thought I would. Finding a true love was once as fantastical to me as magic, but I believe in both now. We were made for each other." Hannah turned and looked up at him then, her eyes full of emotion. "You spent your life creating one thing. Stay with me and create another. A life. With me."

Hannah opened her mouth to answer, but he still had one thing to tell her first.

"The treaty has been extended."

Joy bubbled inside him as he watched her eyes widen in understanding.

"Extended?"

He nodded. "Aye. I heeded your advice, though Walter and I nearly came to blows over it. I surprised Sutherland, and myself, with an offer. To re-sign the treaty on behalf of Kenton and acknowledge our share of the blame for past events. I may have wounded the pride of some of my men, especially those who have spent their lives hating Clan

Sutherland. But nothing, most especially pride, is worth the loss of life."

Once Tristan was confident Hannah fully understood how much he needed her, valued her, he asked the question once again.

"Hannah Sutton . . . will you stay here with me? Love me as I love you?" He took a deep breath. "Will you agree to become my wife when we find your sisters?"

It was a lifetime later when she finally answered.

"No."

---

20

*H*annah knew what she needed to do as soon as she heard his voice. And then he said everything she needed to hear. He truly respected her and saw her as a partner, which was all she'd ever wanted in a man.

Hannah grabbed Tristan's arms as they fell to his sides.

"Nay," she said quickly, not wanting him to misunderstand. "I don't want to wait to marry. We will find Caroline and Allie." They were *here*. She felt it in her bones. "But I love you, Tristan, and I want to marry you right away."

The look of mingled relief and passion in his eyes was her undoing. When he kissed her, it was not the soft, sweet touch from before. This one was hard, demanding. She opened to him immediately, and their tongues dueled in a dance of pent-up desire.

His hands were everywhere at once, and she welcomed the onslaught. Hannah did her best to return the favor, pulling up on the surcoat that ended just above his knees. They lifted it over his head together, and then Tristan disposed of his linen shirt so quickly that Hannah hardly had time to appreciate what was underneath before he pulled her toward him once again.

"I need you, Hannah," he said between kisses, his hands tugging at the sides of her gown. His ability to unfasten the laces while ravishing her with his mouth was something Hannah would take the time to appreciate later.

"I've thought of this so many times," she said when he stepped back to lift the sleeveless overgown above her head.

Tristan looked down at her chemise and smiled. A slow, sly smile that promised neither of them would reconsider. Without protection, there could only be one ultimate outcome here, and Hannah was more than prepared for it. Indeed, she welcomed it.

The sole torch flickered behind Tristan as he began to remove the belt that held his wool chausses. Hannah couldn't look away. "Sometimes," he said, the frantic pace from earlier replaced by a more deliberate one, "I thought of you lying in my bed, naked, waiting for my touch."

His belt came undone.

"Others, I imagined you above me, in control."

And just like that, Tristan was completely, gloriously, nude. And one hundred percent ready. Dear Lord . . .

"Once"—he reached for her chemise—"I woke with the feel of you beneath my hands so real that I was convinced you were with me."

When he pulled the last remaining barrier over her head and tossed it aside, Hannah lifted her chin. If only she'd gone to the gym like she'd been promising herself for the last six months.

"You are perfect."

Had he read her mind?

She certainly wouldn't argue with him. Hannah stepped toward him, pressing every inch of her body against him. Finally. Skin to skin, she kept moving, walking, until the bed was just behind him. In a single, graceful movement, Tristan turned her around, lifted her, and tossed her onto the bed. He kissed her everywhere, his mouth beginning at her neck and ending firmly on her breast. His tongue flicked against her as she tried to pull him even closer.

"Now," she said, not willing to wait any longer. After weeks of frustrating desire, the wait was finally over. She needed to feel him inside her.

"Hmmm," he murmured against her, and with a final soft breath that hardened an already taut nipple, Tristan positioned himself above her. But instead of listening to her plea, he inched his way down, kissing between her breasts and then the top of her stomach.

"I can't take much more," she said, the sight of him positioned above her driving her completely mad. She'd never been a patient person in her private life, even though she could be so professionally, and this was no exception.

"You'll have to try," he said, the deep penetrating tone making her sex clench in anticipation.

He moved lower still, not stopping until his warm breath fluttered her dark curls. Hannah thought she knew what he was about, but he stopped before he reached her apex.

Tristan laid both hands on her upper thighs, staring up at her with a knowing grin that promised the torment would continue. He moved his fingers ever so slightly toward her hips, all the while watching her as she watched him.

What was he doing?

"Close your eyes," he said, moving his hands closer and closer to their goal.

Or at least she hoped it was their goal.

With one last glance at the beautiful sight below her, Hannah did his bidding. "Best not to become accustomed to that outside the bedchamber," she said. "I'm not a fan of taking orders."

Suddenly, his hands were gone and she could feel his breath moving down . . . getting closer. And then he stopped.

"Hannah . . ."

"You're killing me, Tristan."

And he was. She didn't know what to expect next. His fingers, his mouth, or—

Hannah's eyes flew open. He stretched his body back over her in an instant. What a tease!

"Mmmm," he said, his finger slipping inside. "You're ready."

She nearly screamed in frustration. "I told you as much," she said, her hands reaching back to grip something, anything.

He withdrew his fingers and moved up, finally entering her. Gently, slowly, until she could not stand it any longer. Hannah reached around him and pulled Tristan down to her, the movement apparently the only encouragement he needed to thrust inside in truth. He filled her, inch by inch, until they were finally, gloriously, joined at last.

When he began to move, Hannah silently congratulated herself on finding a man who literally had professional training. She didn't even care at the moment how he had come by it. Tristan moved, and she with him, until she finally snapped. Already, her climax was near. When his hand slipped under her, squeezing her buttocks and pulling them toward him, she lost control.

Her pulsating release came hard, squeezing and gripping this man who would be her husband. His groan told Hannah the pleasure wasn't hers alone. With a sound that was all male, all Tristan, he collapsed against her as she reveled in the aftermath of the singular most amazing bout of love-making in the entire world.

Across centuries.

Nothing, not even the promise of a piece of chocolate peanut butter cake, could convince her to leave now.

"WE ARE GETTING MARRIED TOMORROW."

Tristan lay down next to Hannah and attempted to catch his breath. He was not sure precisely what had just happened, but he knew he already wanted it again.

When he looked over, Hannah, lying on her side with her head propped in her hand, was smiling. And the minx was not being shy in her perusal.

"What are you looking at?" he asked, already knowing the answer.

"You."

They needed to talk, but if she kept looking at him that way, nothing would get accomplished this night. In their rush to the bed, they had not bothered with covers. So Tristan remedied that by pulling them down from underneath them and then covering both himself and his intended.

She laughed. "Why in God's name are you doing that?"

He pulled her toward him, also not a very wise idea. They were fully covered now, but the feel of her against him was just as enticing as seeing her luscious curves on full display.

"We need to talk," he answered.

Hannah ran her hand from his shoulder down to his waist, the simple touch stirring his desire. Their talk would need to be short. But he needed to be sure.

"Do you understand what you've agreed to, Hannah?"

Her hand froze, though unfortunately it did so on his buttocks. He squeezed them under her fingers, teasing her and tormenting himself.

"I do," she said, her hand moving dangerously closer.

"You will become the Lady of Saxford—"

"And you will treat me as you do Gerard," she finished.

"Then I should not do this?" He kissed her, innocently enough, until her tongue touched his own.

Tristan pulled back, enjoying seeing Hannah in his bed.

"Certainly not," she teased. "But as a partner," she said more seriously. "I have some ideas on how to make Saxford more efficient, starting with—"

"Save the details for later, partner," he said, placing his finger on her lips. "When we find your sisters, what if they want to leave?" This he said more seriously.

Part of him did not want her to answer, but he had to know Hannah understood the enormity of her decision.

Hannah moved his finger, intertwining their hands.

"I've thought of little else."

She pulled away from him then and laid her head down on the pillow. He'd be content to simply watch her as her lips shifted to the side in concentration.

"*When* we find them . . . if they decide to leave . . ." She sighed, and Tristan wanted to take away her pain. For he could see how difficult such a thing would be for her. Hannah's sisters were her entire world, especially since her parents' accident. "If they decide to leave, I will be heartbroken. But less so than I would be if I left half of my heart here and went back—if such a thing is even possible. There will be challenges, of course, and there's much that I'll miss."

"Such as?"

"Modern medicine. It scares me a bit to know I can't take an antibiotic, or that a midwife will deliver our babies . . ." Hannah's eyes widened. "You do want children? I should have asked that before. I mean, we just—"

"I do," he said. "With you, I do."

He placed his hand on her flat stomach. "We will find the most skilled midwife in all of England, or Scotland."

"Or Allie," she said. "My sister is a nurse."

Tristan couldn't remember Hannah telling him much about her sisters' lives back in Maine. Every time she spoke of them, it was with sadness and regret. That she was talking more of them now, willingly, signaled a more hopeful outlook.

"I'll explain what that is another time."

"You have much to tell me still," he said. "Events that are yet to happen—"

"Technology that you will likely never quite understand."

Hannah gave him a look he recognized. He was in trouble. Sure enough, she let go of his hand and laid it instead on his chest. But it didn't stay there for long.

"You asked if I'd thought this through. If I understood what I was giving up to stay."

As her hand moved downward, Tristan knew their discussion had come to an end.

"But the more important question is, do I know what I am gaining by choosing you? Choosing this century?"

She'd found her mark.

"The answer is yes. Unequivocally, without a doubt. Yes."

Tristan smiled, knowing he had gained as much, if not more, as his love.

EPILOGUE

"*W*hat in God's name do you think you're doing?"

Hannah still marveled over the fact that she'd married a medieval knight, an actual lord who *literally* carried a sword commanded many under him. Less than a fortnight had passed since their hasty wedding, an event that would have made her former self weep for its simplicity. But Hannah was a changed woman. Tristan had just tossed her over his shoulders like a sack of potatoes, something that would have shocked her if she were back home. Now she simply asked a very reasonable question.

"Your favorite epithet," he teased. Tristan ignored her question and continued to carry her up the stairway that led from the kitchen to the courtyard above.

"Cook has had you locked inside there for long enough," he complained.

Hannah tried to raise her head to deny the claim, but she forgot all about her next retort when his hand slipped from her waist to the bare skin just above her leather boot. It moved higher and higher with each step they climbed until it splayed across her thigh, much too high for him to pull it away with any modicum of decorum were they to be discovered.

It was nearly sundown, and while most of the residents of Saxford had already begun to filter into the hall for the evening meal, she'd chosen to skip the ridiculous custom of changing for supper to help Cook with his final preparations for Lord Kenton's visit. Tristan's mentor would be arriving any day to discuss both the peace treaty with Sutherland and, presumably, to congratulate them on their nuptials. Kenton unnerved Cook, which she could understand, and he'd gone into overdrive to ensure all was ready for the overlord's arrival.

"I was just helping him prepare for Kenton," she argued. "Certainly no reason to . . . oh!"

His hand slid even higher, and she could no longer ignore the fluttering inside her stomach. In such an awkward position, Hannah should be concentrating on getting down and preserving her decency, not on anticipating what her husband would do next.

When he lowered her to the ground nearly as abruptly as he'd picked her up, Hannah did protest. Or attempted to protest, at least. Just when she opened her mouth to say something, Tristan took full advantage and slammed his mouth against hers. He kissed her with such force it pushed them both back against the stone wall of the kitchen from which they'd just emerged. Luckily, he'd moved them to the side of the building first, away from prying eyes.

But still . . .

Vague thoughts of teasingly berating him drifted away as a deep longing bubbled up from her core and coursed through every inch of her body. He affected her this way every. Damn. Time. When Tristan planted his hands on the wall behind her, bracketing her head, she pulled him toward her. She only stopped when the evidence of his need was pressed against her.

"My lord . . ."

Groaning, Hannah hid behind Tristan as he pulled his lips from hers. She didn't dare laugh at his expression. Poor Gerard.

"The king," Tristan ground out, his annoyance evident, "and his men better be waiting at the gates." He did not turn to look at the steward. Instead, he watched her, his eyes hooded and his lips still wet from their kiss.

Damn, he was hot.

"We do not know who the riders are, my lord. But a small party is approaching from the north."

Still, he did not turn. His gaze held her in its thrall.

Hannah knew she shouldn't taunt her husband. If she did, she was likely to pay for it later that evening.

That very thought was what made her do it.

Hannah opened her mouth ever so slightly, letting the tip of her tongue rest against her top lip. Then, moving as slowly as she could manage with him looking at her like that, she brought her lower lip into the fold, biting it.

When his low, tortured groan elicited a laugh from her, Gerard cleared his throat.

Tristan finally did turn toward his steward. "Meet them at the gate," he said, the authority in his voice making her even more eager for him. "We will be on the walk."

The wall-walk, he meant, where he could see the riders approach from a safe distance. If he were alone, Tristan would have joined Gerard, but he took more precautions with her safety. And judging from some of the conversations between he and his marshal, such measures were warranted.

Grabbing her hand and winding his fingers through hers, Tristan led her through the courtyard as Gerard hurried away in the opposite direction, toward the gatehouse.

"Do you think Kenton is here early?"

"His colors would have been recognized."

Of course. She still had so much to learn about her new home, her new time.

"So why exactly did you drag me from the kitchen like that?"

She stood a step above him, which meant they were nearly equal in height.

He shrugged. "I wanted you for myself, and it seemed the quickest way to get you away from Cook. And I remembered how easy it was to carry you this way."

Of course. He'd slung her over his shoulders like this on the first day they'd met. She'd passed out after seeing the chaos of Saxford's inner courtyard, incapable of processing that she'd been marooned in medieval England. Though she'd only leapt off Leannan Falls at the urging of her sister Caroline, her reluctance had been due to the height—not to the possibility that the falls were truly enchanted. And yet here she was . . . the jump had landed her nearly on the doorstep of the man she was meant to love.

She took his hand again as they looked out beyond the castle walls to the lush green landscape beyond. Hannah loved to be up here just before the sun set and night blanketed everything. A view, Tristan had pointed out, that would have once terrified her.

But it also reminded her of home. Not Boston, but her true home, the one where she and her sisters had spent so many nights watching the sun set, lying in wait until it was dark enough for them to chase unsuspecting fireflies to fill their jars.

Hannah gave her attention to the riders. As they were about to enter the gates, one of them, a woman, looked up. At first, Hannah thought her mind must be playing tricks on her. Surely the woman riding in front of the dark-haired man only resembled Caroline because she was thinking of her sisters. But as she held the woman's gaze, a joy so over-powering that it nearly brought her to her knees told her what her eyes had not yet completely reconciled.

Her sister Caroline was about to ride into Saxford Castle.

She was going to faint again.

But just as he reached out to catch her, Hannah lifted the hem of her gown and ran back the way they'd come. He followed, calling to her, attempting to learn what—or whom —she'd seen below. But instead of answering, Hannah nearly fell down the last remaining stairs in her haste.

Tristan's hand moved to the hilt of his sword as he followed his wife. She ran toward the newcomers as if . . .

Nay, it couldn't be.

Even if her sisters had fallen through time as she had, how could they have found her so quickly? He'd sent men back to Edinburgh to make further inquiries, and he and Hannah planned to visit the city themselves as soon as Kenton's visit came to an end. But the frantic pace she set . . .

When the visitors came into view, Tristan's eyes found a woman who looked remarkably like his wife, her hair loose and flowing freely. Hannah's shouts told him what he already knew—his instinct had been correct.

"Caro! Oh my God, Caro!"

When Caroline's horse halted and the man she was riding with helped her dismount, Hannah ran up to her and the two women embraced as if . . . as if they'd thought they would never see each other again.

A lump formed in his chest and rode up to his throat. As he watched his wife's reunion with her younger sister, Tristan felt his own eyes fill with tears. He did not wish to disturb Hannah, but he moved closer, choking back the emotion that threatened to overwhelm him.

Tristan glanced at her companion, a Scotsman, and the five other men on horseback. There were six in all, and their plaid was one he'd never seen before. Tristan held his hand out to the man who'd dismounted and now stood by Caroline's side. He would normally wait for Gerard to make the introductions, but the circumstances were anything but normal.

"Tristan, Lord of Saxford and husband to Lady Hannah—"

"You're *married?*" Caroline said as the two men shook hands.

Hannah and her sister broke apart but continued to hold each other's hands. They began talking at once, and the Scot's name was lost in the torrent of words.

"You're here?" Hannah pulled her a little closer, as if she needed the proof of it.

"I thought I would never see you again," her sister said.

"I thought the same. I can't believe you are truly here, at Saxford."

"After we jumped, did you surface in Scotland?"

"No, I woke up here, at Saxford. On the beach just down there." Hannah pointed to the place where they'd first met.

"And how the hell did you get married? When?"

For the first time since she'd spied her sister approaching, Hannah looked at him. Dropping one of Caroline's hands and taking his, she introduced them.

"Caro, this is Tristan. The man who found me."

The sisters exchanged a knowing look.

"I think I understand. This is Callum. He found me, too."

With his free hand, Tristan gestured toward the keep. "Mayhap we should continue this discussion inside."

"That would be wonderful," Caroline said. "But before we do, I have to know—is Allie here?"

Hannah released his hand and turned to face her sister.

"No." Her gaze darted from her sister to the remaining riders. "So you haven't seen her?"

Caroline's brow creased. "No. But based on what we learned at Leannan Falls not long ago, I think she could be here in this time with us."

"Wait. You've been back to the falls too?"

Caroline nodded. "We just came from there. We met the strangest woman. She said I was one of the 'women of the water'—one of the *three* women of the water. Which means Allie could be out there somewhere."

Hannah turned to him. "Do you think that could be the same woman your men met in Edinburgh?"

"Aye, it could be indeed." He shifted his gaze to Caroline. "We returned to the falls not long after Hannah arrived. She jumped in, attempting to go back. Then we sent men to search for information about you and Allison."

The thought of that day still pained him. Sometimes he still awoke from dreams that Hannah had indeed gone back, leaving him forever. But she was always warm in bed beside him.

The Scot spoke then. "That is how we found ye. The woman spoke of men asking about others like Hannah. Saxford men."

"So you have no idea where she is?" Hannah asked.

"No, but I have a feeling she's close. The old woman said that we were brought here to meet our soulmates." She shot a warm glance at the Scot before continuing. "Whether it was fate or destiny or a cursed faerie—" she waved her hand, "—that sounds pretty weird. I didn't understand most of what that woman was saying, but I think whatever force brought us here knows that we couldn't truly be happy without each other."

"So the rumors are true. We heard much the same." Hannah took a deep breath. "When Tristan's men returned, I knew you and Allie had come through the falls. But I still can't believe you're safe and here with me at Saxford."

"We shall find your sister." Tristan would make sure of it.

"Aye," Callum agreed. Their eyes met, and they both nodded, making a silent accord.

"For now, come inside as guests of Saxford—"

"Yes, come. We have so much to catch up on," Hannah said. "And a lifetime to do it in."

THANK you for reading FALLING FOR THE KNIGHT! I hope you loved meeting Tristan and Hannah. Get final book in the Enchanted Falls trilogy, FALLING FOR THE CHIEF-TAIN by Keira Montclair, on Amazon and in Kindle Unlimited.

IF YOU LOVE Scottish historical romance, get THE WARD'S BRIDE, the prequel novella to my Border Series FREE by becoming a CM Insider.

TOO MANY NEWSLETTERS? Get new releases only for future books by following me on BookBub.

FALLING FOR THE CHIEFTAIN: ENCHANTED FALLS BOOK THREE

Allison Sutton isn't the sort to take risks. She's a nurse, so she's seen exactly where risk-taking can lead. But she leaves her comfort zone to visit Scotland with her sisters, and then takes a further leap of faith when one of them insists they jump from a waterfall that's supposedly enchanted. To her amazement, the jump brings her back in time, to the fourteenth century, and she comes face to face with a strapping Highlander who looks as if he's stepped out of her fantasies.

After his brother betrayed him, Brann MacKay has gone out of his way to display his prowess. Which makes it all the more embarrassing when he saves a slip of a lass from a crowd of men, only to earn a kick to the bollocks for his efforts. Even so, Brann is taken with the brash beauty. Allison is like no lass he's ever met, and he quickly realizes why. She emerged from the enchanted pool on his land. She wishes to return to her own world, but her knowledge of healing makes her indispensable to his people—and he quickly realizes *she* is indispensable to him.

Being with Brann makes Allison reconsider her stance on risks, but can a modern woman be happy with a medieval man?

Order Now

FALLING FOR THE HIGHLANDER: ENCHANTED FALLS BOOK ONE

Caroline Sutton doesn't belong here. Not in the Highlands, and certainly not in the fourteenth century.

Headstrong Caroline hopes an adventure will ease the pain of her parents' deaths. One minute, she's standing at the edge of a waterfall, daring her two sisters to jump with her. The next, she wakes up on the shores of a Scottish loch—600 years in the past. She's determined to return to her sisters and her own time, but Callum, the rugged Highland Laird who discovers her, has other ideas. When heat flares between them, all Caroline's plans are thrown into jeopardy, but if she gives in to her blazing desire, she may never want to leave the past behind.

Laird Callum MacMoran is in a bind. He has inherited a clan feud with no end in sight. When he comes across a strange yet strikingly beautiful woman on enemy lands, he thinks to use her as a bargaining chip to end the bloodshed. Little does he know this odd lass is more than she seems, and falling for her will threaten the peace he has worked so long to build. Torn between responsibility to his clan and his growing feelings for Caroline, can he love her enough to let her go? Or will fate decide their futures for them?

Order Now

ENJOY THIS BOOK?

Reviews are extremely important for any author and an essential way to spread the word about the Border Series. There is nothing more important that having a committed and loyal group of readers share their opinion with the world.

If you enjoyed this book, I would be extremely grateful if you could leave a short review on the book's Amazon page. You can jump there now by clicking the link below.

Review Falling for the Knight

ALSO BY CECELIA MECCA

The Border Series
The Ward's Bride: Prequel Novella
The Thief's Countess: Book 1
The Lord's Captive: Book 2
The Chief's Maiden: Book 3
The Scot's Secret: Book 4
The Earl's Entanglement: Book 5
The Warrior's Queen: Book 6
The Protector's Promise: Book 7 (Sept. 2018)
The Rogue's Redemption: Book 8 (Oct. 2018)

ABOUT THE AUTHOR

Cecelia Mecca is the author of medieval and paranormal rom romance, though she sometimes wishes she could be transported back in time to the days of knights and castles. Though the former English teacher's actual home is in Northeast Pennsylvania where she lives with her husband and two children, her online home can be found at Cecelia-Mecca.com. She would love to hear from you.

Stay in touch:
info@ceceliamecca.com